The River Tree

Mairi MacLachlan has brought up four children, worked as a full-time History teacher and also carved out a notch for herself as a novelist.

She has spent a large part of her life in different parts of the world; Scotland, England, Ireland and Canada — but for the past ten years has been based in Inverness-shire. Mairi worked for four years with the BBC writing scripts for programmes such as 'Woman's Hour' and 'Listen with Mother' as well as a number of radio plays.

Her adult novels include *Trumpets for the Brave* based on the aftermath of the Clearances, and *All the Roses Falling* on the life of a Scots family in Belfast.

THE RIVER TREE is her first novel for teenagers.

MAIRI MACLACHLAN

The River Tree

Richard Drew Publishing
Glasgow

First published 1988
by Richard Drew Publishing Ltd
6 Clairmont Gardens, Glasgow G3 7LW
Scotland

The Publisher acknowledges the financial assistance of the
Scottish Arts Council in the publication of this book.

British Library Cataloguing in Publication Data

MacLachlan, Mairi
  The river tree.
  I. Title II. Series
  823′.914[F]

ISBN 0-86267-219-8

Set in Chinchilla by Swains (Glasgow) Limited
Printed and bound in Great Britain by
Cox & Wyman Ltd., Reading

Today is my birthday: today I, Peg Price, am fifteen.

I sit in my favourite place, high up among the branches of the River Tree, and look down at the river itself, running and rippling and glittering below me as it strings through the green Kent farmland towards the Channel coast.

Perhaps Dr Rutland would be angry if he knew I came here; it is his chestnut tree, after all, on his private land.

Stephen, of course, would laugh.

Sometimes, on a summer evening, from where I am sitting now I can see right down the river as far as the estuary, seven miles away. But only sometimes, only if the light is right.

And then — sometimes — while I am watching, the sun dips slowly towards the horizon, and the estuary plunders the light from the sky and transfigures it and flings it back again; a pale lemony light now in the last of the sunset, as tangy as if you could taste it on your tongue, and sharp and needle-cold.

Then a shiver runs through me and sets my mind and body tingling and I sense there is something out there waiting for me, something I don't yet know about, something I can't yet touch or understand; something — what? — that makes me strangely lonely, strangely excited, strangely afraid.

Then the light fades and the River Tree shakes its leaves all round me in a murmuring rustle, and I think: the River Tree knows, the River Tree understands.

And one day, if I can only listen, perhaps it will tell me....

'Somebody cut the lights,' ordered Leonard. He was standing in the middle of the narrow floor. 'Now remember, all of you, it's truth and honour absolutely. Lies are out.'

Dan climbed the ladder and flicked off the switch at the entrance hole. At seven in the evening on the last day of August a sullen sun was still burning from the metallic sky, but here inside the Anderson it was shadowy and cool. We sat crammed together on the two facing benches; behind us steel walls curved into the low steel roof, and the floor under our feet was damp, new-dug earth.

There was new-dug earth on top of the roof too, so that when you saw it from the outside the air-raid shelter looked like a humpy burrow in the ground. Mum said she'd plant flowers on it when she had time, to make it less of an eyesore. But eyesore or not, I thought it was a super place to have a birthday party.

Dan came back to where he'd been sitting opposite me. His face looked lean and secret in the dimness, as if it covered up his thoughts. But that was silly, there was nothing secret about Dan; he lived in a cottage half a mile down the road from us, and I'd known him all my life.

Leonard, on the other hand, was a stranger.

Now Leonard leaned his smooth, seal-like head forward and said in his silky voice, 'No dodging, mind.' His eyes swivelled towards Dan and he added, 'Every single one of us has to answer the question.'

Gooseflesh prickled at the back of my neck and it was suddenly quiet, except for the kitten mewing squeakily in a corner. Tom picked the kitten up and came and sat on the floor in front of me, leaning against my knee. I put an arm round him.

'Here's the question, then,' said Leonard into the silence. *'What scares you most of all?'*

Somebody started to giggle and then smothered the

sound hurriedly.

'Why do you want to know?' I asked.

Leonard raised a snaky eyebrow. 'Chicken, Peg?'

'Certainly not!'

'It's just a game,' said Hazel.

Hazel — my older sister — has a habit of looking for the best in people. I wasn't sure Leonard had a best to look for. We'd only invited him and Joanie because Mum insisted you couldn't leave new neighbours out.

That didn't mean he could run the show.

'Why *do* you want to know?' I challenged him. 'I don't mind telling — well, not much — but first I'd like to know why.'

'Quite right,' said Leonard, approvingly. 'Because it's the quickest way to get to know people, that's why. Take you for instance. Anyone can see what you *look* like. Freckles and a straight brown fringe, and those no-nonsense eyes — an artist would do you in pencil, not water-colours like Hazel.'

'Thanks a lot.'

'Actually you're not badlooking. But that's not the point. You can't really know a person unless you know what makes them tick — And we may not have much time to find out.'

I saw his point. Almost anything might be going to happen now. . . . It sounded a super game.

'All right then,' I said. 'Bridget, you begin.'

Bridget was Dan's sister and my best friend. 'Spiders,' she said, wriggling her plump shoulders. 'Spiders scare me absolutely solid. Whenever I meet one I screech for my dad and he says, "Tell it to wait a minute while I get my gun"—'

Everyone laughed.

'A perfectly normal scare,' nodded Leonard. 'Probably traceable to some folk memory from primeval times, but we needn't go into that. Good for you, Bridget. Now Tom.'

'Kittens getting drowned,' said my brother.

I'd been sure Tom would say that. The kitten was nuzzling under his neck, purring; he and I had managed to coax Dad into letting us keep it, but only on condition it was the last. So next time. . . .

From now on whenever one of the cats got pregnant we'd have to smuggle it into a safe place and look after the cat and its kittens until they were old enough to give away. Then we'd have to find them suitable homes — but it was worth any trouble, Tom said, to save kittens getting drowned.

He cuddled the kitten against his cheek. '*And* that man who always shouts in the cinema,' he added, before it was someone else's turn. 'I think he's really scary. Those *eyes*.'

'He means Hitler,' I explained. 'On the newsreel.'

'A sign of our times,' sighed Leonard. 'Little boys didn't notice the news when I was his age. Eight, aren't you, Tom, the same as Joanie?'

'Nine,' said Tom.

'Nobody can help noticing,' said Bridget. 'What with sandbags all over the place, and every other person measuring windows for Mr Warburton's blackout, or digging trenches in their back gardens.'

Leonard was counting us off on his fingers and muttering names as he slotted us into families: himself and Joanie, Dan and Bridget, Hazel and Tom and me.

'My turn next,' begged Joanie, jigging about on the bench in her impatience. 'I'm scared almost to death of ghosts! I only have to think about them to get lovely shivery feelings inside. . .'

Joanie was enjoying herself. All right if you had scares like that, I thought. Lucky Joanie —

'Now Peg,' said Hazel.

Truth and honour, what scares you most?

But it would sound so silly; and anyway I needed more time to think about it. Perhaps I could say something else instead? Crawly things like Bridget's spiders — centipedes? They did scare me, too, even though I'd been born and bred on a farm.

I said, 'I don't know yet.'

'Everybody knows,' said Leonard.

'I'm scared of never getting married,' Hazel offered. 'Of

4

nobody ever wanting or asking to marry me.'

'Fat chance!' I said enviously. If either of us two was destined never to get married I knew it wouldn't be Hazel. Pretty and serene and kind, with everybody liking her — I wished a bit more of her would rub off on me.

'Hazel doesn't mean she's scared of *nobody* wanting to marry her,' Tom said in a penetrating voice. 'She means *Stephen.*'

'Tom, *shut up!*' I said in horror, and stuffed my hand over his mouth to make him.

Stephen was our landlord's son, and both Hazel and I were in love with him. We'd talk about him for hours in bed at night, and if I'd dared, I'd have invited him to my party. But Stephen was eighteen and at Cambridge, and he didn't notice either of us — not really *notice*, I mean, in the way we wanted.

If Tom had said that about me I'd have burned to a cinder with agonising embarrassment. Hazel didn't answer but she bent her head, and I knew, as clearly as though I could see them, that there'd be tears in her eyes. There were times when I'd get mad at Hazel, but she was my sister; you can't let somebody in your own family be hurt and not try to help. Somehow, I'd got to take the attention off her.

'I think Leonard should tell next,' I said. 'After all, he started this.'

'Yes!' said Joanie. 'Come on, Leonard. You tell them!'

Leonard leaned his head back against the wall of the Anderson shelter, and said in a casual off-handed way, 'Well, I suppose I'm most afraid of failing. Or at least I would be if—'

'—if it ever occurred to you that you might,' interrupted Dan. 'Don't worry, your kind never does.'

I stared at Dan. So I'd been right, after all; there *was* something the matter. Nobody could miss the open hostility in his voice.

And this was the first time he'd spoken since the game began. I peered at his face in the dimness and suddenly I was reminded of another day when Dan acted oddly, a day when he'd gone mad because some of us took an egg out of a starling's nest. There had been five eggs and we'd only taken one; we wanted to start a collection. But Dan had gone mad; he'd called us killers and mindless vandals, he'd shouted at us that birds mattered too, they mattered as much as people. I'd never seen anyone so furious. It was impossible not to be impressed, and none of us had ever gone birdnesting again.

Now Dan's eyes were locked onto Leonard's, and antagonism seemed to spark between them like an electric charge. I didn't want it exploding at my party.

'Come on, Dan,' I said encouragingly. 'Your turn now. Tell us what your worst scare is.'

'Yes, Dan — your turn!' echoed Leonard. He tilted his head to one side and the whites of his eyes gleamed mockingly in the shadowy light.

'You can stuff your silly game,' Dan said shortly. 'I'm not telling.'

'I didn't think you would,' said Leonard. 'Even though it's truth and honour. Even though you promised—'

'I didn't promise anything,' said Dan.

There was an uncomfortable silence. It seemed to me we weren't playing a game any more; Dan had turned it into something different.

After a moment Joanie said, rather breathlessly, 'I've got another scare, too. Worse than ghosts. It's being new at school, and not knowing anybody.'

This time she meant it, she was scared. You could tell by her eyes.

'Don't worry, Joanie,' Hazel said comfortingly. 'Tom will help you get to know the other children. Won't you, Tom?'

Tom twisted suddenly against my arm. 'There's something I'm really scared of, too — I mean, *really* scared. Being sent away. Being evacuated—'

'But Tom, you told us you'd enjoy it!' Hazel protested; she sounded astonished. Sometimes Hazel doesn't see what's in front of her nose. 'You said it would be fun.'

'Yes. I know I did. But now . . .' Tom didn't finish, and I could feel his whole body shaking.

6

'Oh well,' Leonard said, a little awkwardly, 'I don't sup-pose it'll ever actually come to that. To an actual evacua-tion, I mean . . . Now Peg, your go. You're the last.'

I was horribly conscious that everyone was looking at me. 'It's difficult to explain,' I started, and then stopped.

'Try,' said Hazel.

'All right, I'll try. You see, when I was little I was afraid of the dark. Because in the dark you bang into things, you make mistakes. You don't know where you're going—Well, that's how I feel now.' I was floundering a bit. 'Only not about the dark. About *growing up*. It's almost the same thing —'

'How do you mean?' asked Bridget.

'When you're growing up you don't know how you'll turn out. You sort of crash into things — and people — and make mistakes. At least I know I will. Half the time I want to stay the same as I am now forever. And then, the other half I'm excited about it, I want to find out where it is I'm going to in the dark — Well, that's all!' I ended defiantly. 'I can't explain it any better! And I can't help it if you don't understand.'

'I do,' said Dan, so quietly that I wouldn't have heard if he hadn't been sitting opposite me, his face only inches away from my own. 'I understand.'

'Well, well, well!' said Leonard, in a slow teasing drawl. 'Who'd have thought it! You're a deep one, Peg Price!'

And then to my relief Mum's voice came calling to us through the entrance hole, and I didn't have to answer him. It was time to come in for supper.

'Did you notice?' asked Hazel as we climbed out of the shelter. 'Nobody admitted being scared about the war.'

But until this last week the war that everybody said was coming hadn't seemed real to us, in spite of all the pre-parations: old Mr Warburton for instance, stumping round the district with his lame leg and his walking stick, explain-ing about Air Raid Precautions and how to organize the blackout; or Mum with her First Aid classes every Friday night.

Of course there were the air-raid shelters: our Anderson, for instance. It arrived crated in sections, and Dad and Henry spent two days digging a huge hole for it among the cabbages and brussels sprouts, and then setting it up and bolting the bits together. Henry — he was our cowman — even put in electric light.

And gasmasks: everybody had to have one, in a brown cardboard box so if war came you could carry it wherever you went. Mum put them in the cupboard under the stairs with the macs and wellington boots, and sometimes Tom and I shut ourselves in the cupboard and put on our gasmasks and played air raids. The gasmasks smelt funny, all rubbery and dusty at the same time, and they made our voices sound hollow and eerie. They were fun.

And there was conscription. Stephen's brother David had been called up last year. He'd just qualified as an architect, and he was furious. But conscription was only for men over twenty, and it didn't affect us.

And then last week, unexpectedly, the newspapers wore big black headlines about a pact between Germany and Russia, and suddenly even Dad was saying war was inevitable now, a question of 'when' and no longer of 'if'

But today was my birthday, and none of us wanted to think about war.

We climbed up from the shelter, through the hole at the top and out into the daylight, and followed Mum into our big, red-and-white, cheerful farm kitchen.

The table was set with platefuls of delicious food, sausages on little sticks, sandwiches, chocolate biscuits, jellies and a trifle; and in the middle of the table was a birthday cake with pink and white icing and fifteen flickering candles.

'Have you been enjoying yourselves?' Mum asked as she poured lemonade into paper cups. 'Pass round the sausages, Peg. What were you doing?'

'Nothing much,' I said.

'We've been getting to know each other,' said Leonard, and his glance went sliding round our faces.

'Oh good,' said Mum. 'Now I don't want any leftovers, please . . .'

Later I had to blow out the candles.

'Make a wish!' everyone shouted, and I wished.

It wouldn't come true, though. Stephen wasn't inside my reach.

But as the last candle wavered and went out a knock sounded on the back door and there Stephen was, himself, walking into the kitchen as if my wish had made him happen.

I could feel the blood rush up into my face, but it didn't matter. Nobody noticed; they were all looking at Stephen. Stephen was like that.

'Come in, come in!' said Mum cordially.

Stephen often walked into our house, teasing and joking and making himself at home. 'Oh, calamity!' he'd say, picking up my exercise book. 'Peg's got her geometry wrong again. Turn that diagram the other way round, dopey, and you'll see. It's easy!' Sometimes he'd even do it for me.

Now he said, 'Sorry if I'm interrupting something—'

'Of course you're not interrupting,' said Hazel. 'You're just in time.'

She had blushed too, but hers was a soft pink blush that made her even prettier, not an embarrassing scarlet flood like mine.

I hunted for something clever and funny to say, something that might make Stephen notice me properly at last, but nothing whatever came to my mind. All I could manage was, 'Have a piece of cake.'

Stephen took the cake, but he scarcely glanced at it. He was frowning.

'Mrs Price, my mother asked me to come over in case you hadn't heard the news.'

'News?' repeated Mum. She stood absolutely still with an empty sandwich plate in her hand, staring at Stephen across the table. 'We had this morning's paper, of course.

But nothing since.'

Stephen said, 'There's been an announcement on the radio. About the children, Mrs Price.'

We didn't have a radio, though Dad kept saying we ought to get one.

'The government put out an order on the one o'clock bulletin,' Stephen was saying. 'The children's evacuation is to begin first thing tomorrow morning.'

'Oh,' said Mum. 'Oh, Tom. . . .'

She looked shocked.

Tom was stuffing cake into his mouth as if he hadn't heard a thing.

Mum said, 'I'd better pack his suitcase. . . .'

I couldn't take it in, I didn't want to. 'It isn't fair!' I said fiercely. 'Why should they make little kids go away — leave their families and go to live with strangers — when the war hasn't even begun?'

'*Has* it begun?' Hazel asked Stephen.

'No. Not yet. Soon.'

Soon. . . .

Everything safe and familiar was crumbling away. I felt hollow and rather sick.

Tom said, 'I'll be all right, Mum,' and added, after a moment, 'I expect.'

Then he got down from his chair and walked round the table to where Mum was standing and leaned against her, and she held him with both arms.

'Thank you for letting us know,' she said to Stephen. 'And thank your mother, too. It was kind of you both.'

She sounded as if someone had wound her up with a key, like a toy, and the words were coming out mechanically.

Joanie butted into the conversation excitedly, bobbing up and down in her chair. 'Tom and I can go together! Can't we, Tom?'

But Tom just turned his back on her and burrowed his head into Mum's blue dress.

'Eat up, all of you,' Mum said, still in that odd mechanical voice. 'No sense letting good food go to waste.'

But nobody seemed to have much room for birthday cake after all. I slipped most of mine to our black collie, Shep, who was lying under the table.

3

We sat on the slippery leather seat in the back of the taxi; Mum and I in the corners and Tom in the middle between us. I wanted to rage at her, 'Why, why? I don't understand! It isn't right to send a little boy away like this! War is supposed to be about soldiers, not about children!'

But I knew it wouldn't have been any use.

'After all they do know what they're doing, Peg,' Hazel had said last night as we lay talking round and round it in bed. 'If the Government think children should be evacuated from here, and Mum and Dad think so too — well, they know best! That's all there is to it.'

'I suppose so,' I admitted wearily. There wasn't much point arguing over anything so obvious. 'All the same, Tom'll be homesick. He'll miss us terribly. . . .'

And there wasn't a single thing I could do about it.

'That's better than being bombed,' said Hazel.

Bombs! Crashing out of the sky onto our town, our farm — However hard I tried I couldn't imagine it.

Things like that happened in books, in newspapers, on the newsreels in cinemas. They didn't have anything to do with our ordinary, predictable, everyday life; things like that didn't happen to us. My mind couldn't produce a picture of the bedroom I shared with Hazel, wrecked and shattered by a bomb.

And even if it did happen, even if the unimaginable came true and we *were* bombed, would Tom really think he was better off separated from the rest of the family, away from our home, *evacuated*?

I was glad Dad had said they couldn't do without my help on the farm, or Mum might have made me be evacuated too.

And now it was September 1st, and the sun, even at nine o'clock in the morning, was blisteringly hot. My bare legs stuck to the leather taxi seat. I stared out of the window at the trees just beginning to turn, at the scattering of pale gold leaves among the green. Conkers too, fattening nicely. I hoped there would be conkers where Tom was going, and Guy Fawkes when November came.

My throat ached from holding back the tears.

Mum had pinned a brown luggage label with Tom's name, written on it in her large round handwriting, to the pocket of his blazer. The government had told her to do that, of course. As if Tom was a parcel.

The train was already half full when we arrived at the station, and dozens of children were standing about on the platform, wearing labels like Tom's and clutching suitcases that looked too big to belong to them. Teachers hurried up and down like sheepdogs, chasing children into groups, herding them into the train; mothers with lost-looking smiles watched from the back of the platform or talked through windows to boys and girls already packed inside the waiting carriages. A child with a runny nose wailed that she had to go to the toilet.

The air smelled clammily of steam and engine oil.

A teacher came over to us and checked Tom's name off her list.

'Well Tommy, isn't this interesting!' she began with earnest cheerfulness. 'Now Mrs Price, you mustn't worry about him at all. I promise we'll take just as good care of him as you would yourself—'

Her voice was cut off, drowned in the deafening high-pitched shriek of the engine as it let off steam. The child with the runny nose burst into sobs, and the teacher looked harassed.

She tried again, shouting to make herself heard. 'I'll write as soon as we get our billets. Our billets — you know, as soon as we've been allocated to the families we'll be staying with—' The engine stopped shrieking and her face went bright red. 'Oh — that's better! My goodness, I'll soon be quite hoarse . . . Sorry, Mrs Price, what was that you said?'

'Tom,' Mum said again, firmly. 'We never call him

13

Tommy.'

'Oh good,' said the teacher. 'Now Tommy — Tom — get your gasmask and your suitcase and come along. No time to waste!'

Something came charging into me from behind and almost knocked me off balance. 'Sorry, sorry, sorry!' said a high, excited voice.

It was Joanie. She made a grab for Tom's arm.

'Oh, *here* you are, Tom! I've been looking for you everywhere! Can I sit next to you on the train? You'll never guess what I've got!' She dug into the scarlet string bag dangling from her wrist to show him. 'Look, comics and chewing gum and toffees and two bottles of lemonade! You can share them if you'll let me sit next to you, I promise—'

Joanie at least was delighted about being evacuated, I thought. And she wouldn't be the only stranger in her new school, after all.

Her mother came pounding up the platform behind her, a tall fat woman with a fat suitcase that looked as if it might burst its straps at any moment. 'Don't run away like that, Joanie! I nearly lost you!'

'Mrs Colfax?' enquired the teacher. 'Oh, good. That's my little lot, then.' She ticked off the last name on her list with a sigh of relief. 'Come on, children! Give your mothers a kiss and say goodbye.'

Tom was too big to kiss people in public. He jerked his head in what he meant to look like a casual farewell and followed the teacher, with his suitcase in one hand and Joanie still attached to his other arm. Once or twice he looked back at us over his shoulder and put down his suitcase and waved.

'I'm sure they'll be all right,' said Mum. 'I'm sure they will. Oh dear, I don't remember packing his slippers, or his dressing gown—'

'You did,' I said. 'Honestly.'

'It was such a rush,' said Mrs Colfax in a plaintive voice. 'Such a terrible rush. We very nearly missed the bus!'

'Oh, how awful of me,' Mum said. She sounded horrified,

14

and tears gathered in her eyes. 'I'm so sorry, I never thought. I should have asked you to share our taxi. I'm terribly sorry Mrs Colfax, I really am!' The tears spilled over and she brushed them away impatiently with her hand.

I couldn't understand her. Tom was going away and we didn't know where, we didn't know when we'd see him again — and here she was getting into a state because she hadn't asked someone we'd hardly met to share a taxi. As if Mrs Colfax mattered more than Tom.

All my hurt and anger boiled suddenly over into furious words. 'It isn't fair!' I lashed out at them both. 'I don't see why Tom has to go away, or Joanie, or any of them! Everywhere else they're sending evacuees *into* the country, not away from it. I don't see what's dangerous about living on a farm—'

'Oh, Peg,' Mum said helplessly. I noticed the dark patches under her eyes and the droop of her shoulders; she looked tired to the bone. 'It isn't because of the farm or the country,' she said. 'Don't you see, Peg, it's because we live so near the coast. Only a few miles across the sea from France, if the Germans should ever get as far as that . . .'

'They never will,' said Mrs Colfax, fiercely.

The children were all on board the train now. Mothers and fathers stood about the platform waiting; on the clock hanging above the ticket-gate the big hand jolted forward to the final minute. Porters slammed the doors shut one by one, a whistle blew; the guard dropped his flag.

The long green train began to move slowly forward, clanking, settling into its rhythm, gathering speed; curving away from us round the bend in the track like a long green hairy caterpillar; the hairs were hands, waving from every window.

Then the train and the children were gone. Only the rails were left, empty and shining in the sun.

When we reached home we found old Mr Warburton sitting in the kitchen with Hazel and waiting for us impatiently.

He wore his ARP helmet and an air of cheerful vigour. The blackout had been ordered to begin at dusk this evening, he told us, his eyes newly brisk and young in his seamy face and his voice brimful of energy; Germany had invaded Poland, and we must be ready for an air raid at any moment.

'So unless you've got your blackout curtains properly rigged by sunset, Mrs Price, you'll just have to manage without lights,' he concluded his instructions. 'You mustn't allow a single chink of light to escape. The enemy can spot a match flame from twenty thousand feet.'

He rolled out 'the enemy' with relish in every syllable; like Joanie, I thought, Mr Warburton was enjoying himself.

'Oh dear,' said Mum, looking flustered.

'We'll help you, Mum,' said Hazel. 'You've made the curtains already, after all. It's just a matter of hanging them up.'

'*And* nailing them in to the sides of each window,' said Mr Warburton. 'You mustn't forget the sides. That's where the chinks appear.'

'Yes,' said Mum. 'Of course.'

One good thing, putting up the blackout would help take our minds off Tom.

'I hope you've managed to get the trench dug to your Anderson?' Mr Warburton went on, leaning forward in his chair with both hands on the silver top of his walking stick. His eyes seemed to skewer Mum's attention.

'Not yet, actually—'

'Then mind you get your husband on to it immediately. Today, that's my advice. And whatever you do don't let anyone leave the house without a gasmask.'

'But surely, we aren't at war yet?'

'Only a matter of hours,' said Mr Warburton sternly. 'The government can't get out of it any longer. Well, I must go and check up on these new people down the road. Remember now, blackout and trench, Mrs Price!'

He hobbled away on his walking stick, almost hopping with energy and enthusiasm.

Mum and Hazel and I spent the rest of the morning hanging up blackout curtains all round the house.

It had taken Mum weeks to make the curtains, out of ugly black material that had been specially supplied to the shops, and which nobody in their senses would have chosen for curtains if they hadn't been forced to. We hammered them into the sides of each window as Mr Warburton had directed, and then hung our own curtains in front of them; the rooms didn't look quite so awful after that.

My arms ached with reaching up, and with each window the day felt hotter, the curtains heavier.

'Sit down and have a rest, Peg,' Mum said after a while. 'You look all in.'

So did she, but she didn't sit down or rest.

The *Daily Express* was lying on the kitchen table. I glanced through it, turning the pages. It was full of things that had happened yesterday and already seemed out of date.

Children were to be evacuated, the Fleet had been mobilized and was ready for war; the last of the reservists had been called up for the armed services.

Guilt stabbed at me suddenly.

Henry! He was one of those reservists. He'd left last night for the Navy; for the war.

Henry, who had always been around for as long as I could remember, who'd taught me how to milk a cow, who'd made a wheelbarrow out of an old wooden box and the wheels from Tom's pram for us to play with; who'd stayed up all night less than a week ago over a difficult calving. Henry, who was part of our lives.

And in all the upheaval of Tom's departure I hadn't found more than a few moments to wish him good luck.

Dad, when he came in for dinner a little while later, was missing Henry already.

'Just when they tell you farming is a top priority and you're expected to produce more than ever before, you lose half your labour force,' he grumbled, helping himself from the bowl of new potatoes in the middle of the table. Then he added, very deliberately, 'Well, girls, this is where you come in. I want you two to take over responsibility for the milking.'

'Oh, *Dad*!' I shouted, hardly able to believe I'd heard right. He'd really meant it when he said he needed me on the farm!

'It'll be easy,' said Hazel, sounding as pleased as I was. 'Milking is nothing with the new machine. You just clip the cups to the cows' udders and switch on—'

'And anyway, we can both milk by hand if the machine breaks down,' I added proudly.

'I'll take on the dairy,' said Mum. She had brightened too, and for the first time that day the tiredness was dispelled from her eyes.

Perhaps everyone feels better if they have an important job to do, and know they're needed.

Perhaps that was why Mr Warburton had seemed so cheerful about the war.

After dinner Dan and Bridget came over, and then Leonard, and they helped us dig a trench from our house to the Anderson.

Leonard, of course, knew exactly how it ought to be done.

'It was the first job we tackled when we moved in,' he told us. 'You really should dig it deeper than that, Mr Price. Five feet deep at least. And of course it should be brick-lined.'

'I haven't got any bricks,' said Dad. 'We'll have to do with wooden planks instead.'

'Bricks would be better,' said Leonard.

He turned out to be quite good at handling a spade all the same, as even Dan unwillingly admitted, and late next afternoon — Saturday — the trench was finished.

'Thanks, everybody,' Dad said as he looked round the circle of flushed and dirt-streaked faces. 'You've done a real job of work. Now go in and get some lemonade and call it a day.'

The weather had got steadily hotter and hotter until now

it felt stifling, with the sun flaring nakedly down at us from a sky of dusty blue.

'There's still the milking,' I remembered, groaning.

'I couldn't!' said Hazel. 'There isn't a single inch of me that doesn't ache after all that digging. I simply couldn't do another thing except sit down and *flop*.'

I knew how she felt because I felt exactly the same. But you can't duck out of a responsibility once you've taken it on; that's the whole point. 'It's our job,' I said crossly. 'It seems to me you were pleased enough about it yesterday—'

'Stop squabbling,' said Dad. 'I'll take care of the milking tonight. You youngsters have had enough.'

But Dan, it turned out, hadn't. He stayed on after Bridget and Leonard had gone home and gave Dad a hand with the milking, and Mum asked him to stay to supper. After that he helped her carry the stores out to the Anderson; tins of milk and biscuits and candles and a camping stove and extra blankets. There wasn't much use having a trench and a shelter, Mum said, if we were going to starve when we got there.

When they'd finished we all went down and inspected the shelter.

It was almost cosy. Scarlet travelling rugs covered the two benches, and there was a store of food in one corner; on a small table at the far end Mum had put books and playing cards and the old gramophone from the attic and some records. I couldn't quite stamp out a wriggling little wish that we might actually get a chance to use the Anderson; it needn't be *much* of a raid, of course, but enough for us to cook on the camping stove and listen to the records from Snow White, or the Teddy Bears' Picnic. . . .

Then we climbed up the ladder out of the shelter again and followed each other along the trench. It was dark now, a thick heavy darkness without a star showing, and the blackout was working perfectly. The house didn't yield a single chink.

Mr Warburton would have been proud of us.

And suddenly, over our heads, a gigantic crash exploded

across the sky.

'Oh my goodness—' Mum gasped, and then together Hazel and I began to laugh. It was thunder; not an air raid, after all.

Lightning forked in jaggy patterns through the darkness and then the rain came, pelting and pouring and hammering down as if it would never stop, tap-dancing on the tin roof of the barn and collecting in runny puddles where the cartwheels had worn narrow channels in the ground; spilling down in spurting rivulets onto the wooden planks lining the brand-new trench.

'Get inside quickly before you're soaked!' Mum said, scrambling out of the trench and opening the kitchen door. Light blazed out into the blackness as Dad followed her in.

But Dan and Hazel and I stayed out there laughing in the rain and let it run down our hair and our faces and our clothes and into our shoes, washing away with it the heat and the tiredness and the feeling of apprehension that had hung like a smoky cloud over that whole day and the day before. I felt clean now, almost confident. The future was rushing towards us like an express train; and there was nothing more we could do to get ready for it, nothing at all.

As we went into the house at last the phone was ringing. Mum went to answer it in the hall.

'That was Tom,' she said when she came back to the kitchen. 'He says he's staying with a lady called Mrs Harrison and she has a moustache and he's in Cornwall. He was sick twice on the train and he's had sausages and cream buns for tea. . . .'

She was crying and laughing, both at the same time.

4

Stephen arrived at our door soon after ten next morning with a message from his mother.

'She wondered if you'd like to come over and listen to the radio. The Prime Minister is going to make a special announcement at a quarter past eleven.'

'War,' said Dad.

It was Sunday, and we were having a late breakfast after milking.

'Please thank your mother, Stephen,' Mum said. 'Yes. We'll all come.'

After Stephen had gone she sat on at the table, not doing anything, simply staring out of the window. The thunder had travelled far away and taken yesterday's steamy swelter with it. Through the kitchen window the red barn roof and the slice of blue sky above it looked as clean as if they'd been scrubbed and polished, but though Mum sat staring at them with her hands lying in her lap she didn't, I thought, see them at all but something else, something terrible and strange. After a bit she sighed and said, 'Who'd have believed that after only twenty years we'd be at war with Germany all over again. . . .'

'Come on,' Hazel whispered to me. 'If we're going to the Rutlands' we'd better get ready.'

I sat on my bed and watched while Hazel brushed her hair and put on her prettiest dress. It was blue cotton, with a tightly fitting waist and a full skirt embroidered with tiny yellow flowers; I zipped her into it and she tied a blue velvet ribbon over the top of her head and under her hair at the back, in a snood.

She looked lovely.

There wasn't much I could do to compete, so I stayed in my old red shorts and gym shoes and pretended I couldn't see what all the fuss was about.

None of us had ever been inside the Rutlands' big white

house before. We sat down on the squashy furniture — a sofa and *three* armchairs, upholstered in bright chintz covers — and tried not to stare too hard at everything all round us. The walls were painted white too, and there were bowls of roses, and photographs of the family in silver frames. One was of Stephen as a baby, fat and sweet and laughing, and somehow even at that age recognizably Stephen. When Stephen looked like that, I wasn't even born, and nor was Hazel.

Someone was playing organ music on the radio. We sat listening to it, and trying to make conversation, and waiting for eleven-fifteen.

'Bad business,' Dr Rutland said, knocking out his pipe on the fender. 'Never thought it would actually come to war. Not after the last time.'

Dad cleared his throat. 'In a way it's almost a relief.'

'Oh, but then you haven't—' began Mrs Rutland, but the doorbell interrupted her and she went off to answer it.

They'd invited the other people who lived nearby as well, I realised with relief; the Skerries — Bridget and Dan and their parents — and the new people, Mr and Mrs Colfax and Leonard. They came in, looking nearly as embarrassed as Dad, and Hazel and I got up off the squashy sofa to make room for the grown-ups.

Stephen took Hazel over to the windowseat, and Bridget and I sat on the white hearthrug, hugging our knees.

And then the radio announcer was saying, 'The Right Honourable Neville Chamberlain,' and the Prime Minister began to speak.

Dad was right, of course. We were at war with Germany.

I glanced round at all the listening faces.

There were tears in Mum's eyes, and Mrs Rutland's elegant pale gold head was bent forward. Nobody moved.

'It is evil things we shall be fighting against,' the Prime Minister said in his tired, sad voice. 'Brute force, bad faith, injustice, oppression and persecution. And against them I am certain that the right will prevail.'

The National Anthem crashed into the silence: God Save

the King.

Mrs Rutland got up out of her chair and stood to attention, and then the rest of us stood up too. Somehow it seemed the natural thing to do at such a moment, it seemed to express what each one of us was feeling.

When it was over we sat down again and I wondered what in the world anyone could say after that.

It was Mrs Rutland who spoke first. 'You must be missing Tom terribly, Mrs Price. And you, Mrs Colfax, your little girl — poor children, poor children.'

'Yes,' said Mum. 'But it isn't as bad as having sons of military age.'

'No,' said Mrs Rutland. 'It isn't.'

Conscription. They'd bring the age down to eighteen now, I thought, and Stephen would have to go as well as David. And Dan and Leonard; they'd both be eighteen in a few months too. But perhaps the war wouldn't last as long as that. . . .

Once Mum had told Hazel she'd had a young man who was killed fighting in France in the last war. I'd never really thought before what that meant. That young man must have been someone like Stephen or Dan.

Stephen looked as if someone had wound up a spring inside him. 'Oh, *calamity*!' he said with relish. 'Here - we - go! And what do you bet the Navy beats Cambridge for a bit of fun and excitement!'

Leonard and Stephen began to laugh.

Dan didn't laugh. His jaws were clamped shut, and he was frowning.

Hazel sat quietly, not saying anything, just looking at Stephen.

What would happen to this group of people, I wondered; all of us who had sat listening to the Prime Minister's broadcast together here in the Rutlands' beautiful drawing room, where would we all be and what experiences would have come to each of us by the time this war that was just beginning reached its end?

And then the siren started. Quietly at first, a low eerie

whine that climbed and climbed till it hit the high note and then dropped again, and went on, up and down, up and down, in an urgent banshee wail. We'd heard it before, of course — only, this time, it wasn't a practice.

'Well I'm damned,' said Dr Rutland. 'They're at it already. Blast their guts!'

'We'll have to go down to the shelter,' said his wife. 'At once — hurry, everybody! Oh dear,' she added, looking round us in consternation, 'you haven't got your gasmasks!'

'Never mind that,' said Dr Rutland briskly. 'Not even Hitler would be stupid enough to use gas. He knows we'd retaliate.'

'Perhaps we ought to go home,' said Mum. 'Just in case.'

I wondered if she was really nervous about gas, or if she'd had about enough of sitting talking politely with the Rutlands and wanted an excuse to get back to our own homely kitchen — or anyway, our own Anderson.

'No, no,' said Dr Rutland. 'They'll be overhead any minute. No sense taking risks,' and he chased us cheerfully out of the room. It occurred to me that Dr Rutland was meeting air raids with almost as much gusto as Mr Warburton.

I was shivering a little, myself, in spite of the warm day. The shiver was half excitement, half apprehension; I couldn't quite believe that any of this was real. Air raids and bombs *were* things that happened to other people in other countries — weren't they? To people in foreign places with funny foreign names — surely nothing like that could happen to us, here, in ordinary everyday old England?

Mrs Rutland scooped up the three gasmasks that dangled from the hatstand in the hall, and we all filed through the glass front door and down through the trench in the back garden (brick-sided, just like the Colfaxes') to the Rutland's Anderson.

It wasn't any different from ours, except that with all that crowd packed into it there was hardly room to breathe. Perhaps that was why Dad's face looked so red.

'On my knee, Peg,' said Stephen. 'You can't weigh more

than a chicken.'

I couldn't believe it.

I wished the raid would last for hours and hours. Once I glanced round at him, and he was laughing. 'Scared?' he teased.

'Oh no.' But I couldn't tell him that the reason for my heart bumping so hard was sheer unbelievable happiness, so I said, 'Well, perhaps a bit,' and he laughed again.

'When the raid's over we'll all go down the river in my boat,' he promised. 'We'd better make the most of everything while we can.'

Hazel heard from where she was sitting on the opposite bench, under the silvery curving roof. She cheered up and smiled at him mistily across the shelter.

After a while the all clear sounded, one long shrill note on the siren without any ups or downs, like a dog howling. The fact was, we learned next day, there hadn't been a single enemy plane over England and the whole thing was a false alarm. We didn't have a proper raid for months and months.

In the afternoon Stephen kept his promise and took us out in his boat: Dan and Bridget, Leonard and Hazel and me.

Stephen's father helped us clamber into *Excalibur* from the small wooden jetty at the end of the Rutlands' garden.

'Careful, now!' he said, smiling at Hazel as he handed her aboard. 'Sit down, everyone, and do exactly as Stephen tells you. As if you're under naval orders!'

Excalibur was painted yellow, with white sails, and before Dr Rutland bought her, a few months earlier, she'd been used for day fishing off the Scottish coast. Stephen planned to race her next season. There was more space in her, I thought now, than I'd realised when I'd watched Stephen and his brother, or sometimes Stephen and Dan, practice with her on the river.

We could have made room for Tom and Joanie as well. Tom would have loved it. . . .

We pushed off, puttering into midstream on the outboard

engine. Dan was steering.

And looking back I could see the River Tree, my River Tree, old and strong and beautiful, standing like a sentinel keeping guard over the river, with the wind rustling secrets in its leaves.

Green fields, broad and peaceful, stretched on either side of us, and there were hops ready for picking on thick green bines, and cattle grazing. It looked an ordinary day like any other. But it wasn't. . . .

'It's so beautiful,' said Hazel. She'd changed her dress for blue slacks and a sweater and she looked as slender and fragile as a flower. I envied her. I loved her, too. Love and envy, both at the same time, boiling up into a pain that gnawed inside me — 'Let's agree to look back and remember what we were doing today, shall we?' she went on. 'Say in six months' time?'

'I'll be in the Navy by then,' Stephen said. 'I'm going to join up tomorrow.' He laughed as she said quickly, 'Oh, *Stephen*—' and then he added, 'Well, that's what one does do in a war, isn't it — join up? You could join the Wrens.'

Hazel nodded, blushing.

'I'm still trying to decide,' said Leonard. 'What to join, I mean. I think it'll be the RAF. That is if the war lasts until my birthday.'

'Lucky things,' said Bridget. 'You'll get all the fun. While Peg and I have to stick at boring old school and miss the exciting bits—'

'Perhaps it'll last long enough for us to join up too,' I said. 'Three years!' It seemed an unimaginably long time. 'Of course there is the St John's Ambulance and the ARP. I suppose we could join them while we wait.'

'Yuck!' said Bridget. 'Housewives and old gentlemen!'

The river broadened out into the estuary and then the open sea, shimmering and glinting under the blazing sheeny sun. Gulls squawked and flapped behind us and Bridget threw them scraps of tomato sandwiches; the air smelt of salt and seaweed and engine oil and the boat rose and dipped, rocking in the long waves off-shore.

'Right,' said Stephen. 'You can cut the engine now, Dan, and we'll sail round the point to the pier.' His glance ranged over each of us in turn, and settled on me. 'Peg, get up there forrard and give me a hand with the jib.'

'Forrard' — 'jib?' I hadn't an idea what he was talking about, but roaring tigers couldn't have made me admit it. Stephen was pointing to the front of the boat; I scrambled past Bridget and Leonard and Hazel, and all of them, I knew for certain, were wishing they'd been asked instead of me.

'You helm, Dan,' Stephen said. 'We'll teach young Peg a bit about sailing, shall we? Just pull that rope, Peg — that's the jibsheet. Pull till those wrinkles in the sail disappear, and the telltales are flying horizontally. That's it! Now hold her steady. And the rest of you sit still and don't do anything idiotic.'

'As if we would,' said Bridget indignantly.

'You might,' said Dan. 'Don't let the jib flap, Peg!'

So the jib was the small sail, then. So far so good.

'Right, Peg!' called Stephen. 'Ready to go about?'

'*What*?'

'Go about. We're going to turn. We'll be sailing across the wind, in the other direction.'

'Why?' I asked. I might as well understand what I was meant to be doing.

'Well, the wind's against us. We have to zigzag to get to the right place.'

'Oh,' I said. 'Okay. Tell me what to do.'

'Hold as you are. . . . Now, when I give the word, you yank the jibsheet out of the cleat — that thing holding it at the side — let it go loose, and duck. Otherwise you'll crack your head on the boom. *Now*, Peg!'

I did exactly as he said. For a second or two the jib flapped loosely, and then I realised why he'd said duck, because the whole jib on its wooden pole — boom — swung right across me as the boat turned. . . . I mean, came about.

'Pull hard on the other jibsheet,' Stephen shouted. 'Pull! Let the sail fill! That's it. . . . Now, clip the sheet into the cleat on that side. The cleat, Peg, think what you're doing — that's it — Good!'

The boat bounded forward, and Stephen and Dan were both grinning at me.

'Well done, Peg!' Dan called, through the arching spray.

I sat there rehearsing the whole sequence in my mind. I was determined that next time Stephen wouldn't have to tell me what to do, I'd get it right on my own.

'Such a lovely name for a boat, *Excalibur*,' Hazel said dreamily. 'So tremendously romantic. . . .'

'Never heard it before,' said Bridget.

'Oh, you must have. It was King Arthur's sword, you know, given to him by the Lady of the Lake—'

'Move over to the other side please, Hazel,' said Stephen. 'We've got too much weight to starboard.'

Hazel moved, looking a bit put out.

'Not tactful,' sighed Leonard, tilting his head towards Stephen. 'Never mind. Some people aren't. Go on about *Excalibur*, my sweet.'

Hazel flushed. 'Yes, well, when Arthur died they threw his sword back into the lake and a hand rose up out of the water and grasped it —'

'Ready to go about, Peg,' said Stephen.

'Ready —'

'Right!'

Excalibur came round with a smooth swinging momentum like the sensation of smashing a tennis ball right in the centre of your racket, clean and accurate. Stephen laughed. 'That's the ticket, Peg. . . .'

The sun shimmered and sparkled on the water and the wind sang, and except for the ache of missing Tom I was entirely, absolutely happy, with a sparkling happiness like the water and the sun.

'Next time, Stephen, will you let me take the jib?' asked Hazel. Evidently she'd given up on King Arthur.

'If there is a next time,' said Stephen.

The pier was packed with people. Some of them leaned on the rail and watched us as we tacked to and fro, making our way towards them.

'Ready about, Peg,' called Stephen.

'Ready. . . .'

Over and over again. . . .

'Never knew anyone pick it up faster,' said Stephen. 'The girl's a natural. Great stuff, Peg!'

By the time we reached the estuary again on our way back, I felt as if I'd been crewing a sailing dinghy all my life.

'Was it wicked of me to have enjoyed today so much?' I asked Hazel, as she put out the light on the table between our two beds. 'After all, the day when war was declared —'

'I'm not sure,' she said cautiously.

I thought about the tears in Mum's eyes this morning, and Mrs Rutland's expression as she looked at Stephen, who was old enough to be called up. All over England, all over Britain, there must have been people crowding round radio sets as we had done in the Rutlands' drawing room, listening, while our country went to war.

'It seems awful to be happy when at the same time terrible things may be going to happen.'

'Perhaps it's the other way round,' said Hazel. 'Perhaps we ought to make the most of everything as much as possible, as long as we can. Like Stephen said.'

But I thought she sounded wistful, and rather sad.

5

After the flurry and drama of the last few days of peace, the war, now that it had arrived at last, turned into anticlimax. Nothing at all happened: there were no enemy planes roaring overhead, no bombs, no blitzkreig, nothing. Nobody used the trench we'd dug so hurriedly, and the tins and biscuits and blankets stayed undisturbed in the shelter.

Even the blackout soon turned from a novelty into a nuisance. It was astonishing how thick the darkness outside the house appeared, how unfamiliar the places you knew best suddenly became when you had to grope your way round them, stubbing your toes and skinning your fingers on unexpected obstacles. Bridget's father missed the turning to their house altogether after coming to see Dad one night, and wandered around in the dark for half an hour before he found his way. And then Mum tripped over a hayrake someone had knocked down in the farmyard, and sprained her ankle badly.

The doctor made her rest for two days with her foot propped up on a cushion, and Hazel and I had to do the dairy work as well as the milking. Just as well, Dad said, that the school had been closed temporarily for 'reorganization'.

'I thought war would at least be exciting,' I grumbled as we mucked out the cowshed. 'Why the silly animals can't wait till they're out in the field— Well, war isn't exciting, it's boring. And I hate cows.'

I didn't, of course, but now my legs ached and my arms ached and I was tired and cross. 'I wish we had Henry back,' I said.

'I wish the war hadn't started,' said Hazel.

She was thinking about Stephen, I could tell. We hadn't seen him once since the boat trip. Even Dan and Bridget didn't come round as much as usual. Perhaps they were being kept busy at home, too.

Then Mum's ankle recovered and school opened again

and our days got back to having a recognizable shape. And there was a letter from Tom.

The war had changed school.

Sandbags were piled up against the outside walls and strips of brown paper had been glued across the windows; stirrup pumps and buckets of water stood in every classroom and corridor, even in the cloakrooms and on the stairs, and large red notices with black lettering said 'Carry Your Gasmask Everywhere!'

But it was more than that. There was a new atmosphere: sharp, purposeful, different.

Miss Miller stood on the platform in the Assembly Hall that first morning and looked down at us as we waited to find out what she would say. She didn't smile or welcome us back. She simply announced the hymn: 'I vow to thee, my country.'

The singing tingled, as if patriotism was beating in the blood in every vein, in every person there.

Then Miss Miller said a prayer for victory in our just cause, and for God to defend the right. She sounded strong and absolutely sure; we were right, so we would win. Like the Prime Minister, I thought, Miss Miller had no doubts about that.

Outside the windows of the hall, crisscrossed with long brown paper strips in case of bomb blast, the sun broke free from the clouds and flooded in over the rows of girls in blue gymslips and white blouses, and suddenly I felt strong and confident too, like Miss Miller.

Then Assembly was over and we filed out of the hall to lessons.

It didn't take long to get used to the new conditions.

There were four air raid practices in the first week. Each time the klaxon sounded (a thin tinny screech like a miniature siren) we had to put on our gasmasks and duck down behind the desks, pretending a bomb had exploded in the playground.

The gym had been commandeered as an ARP station, and

we couldn't use it. Instead of PE we had First Aid, practising making splints and putting on bandages. That was fun.

Classes were different too, telescoped together or even dropped from the timetable because nearly a quarter of the school had been evacuated, and some of the teachers were already in the Services. It was a bit unsettling, but interesting. And all the time there was a feeling of waiting, of expectancy; nobody knew, nobody could guess, what might happen next.

Few of the teachers minded getting side-tracked from work to talk about the war. Would Germany gobble up Belgium, once she'd digested Poland? Would she invade France — or even England?

'Not England, no, not at all,' Mademoiselle said positively. Mademoiselle wore delicious-smelling perfume, and thick black mascara on unbelievably long eyelashes. She was young and pretty and excitable, and getting her excited made French a lot better fun than history or maths. With luck and skill, getting Mademoiselle excited could put off *dictée* almost indefinitely.

'Not England,' she repeated now, her eyes stormy. 'You English are safe as long as my country is fighting still, and we will never, never give in to *les sales Boches—*'

'That's not quite what you told us before,' said Felicity. 'Remember 1871.'

'And I don't think you should call the Germans dirty,' said Annabelle. In contrast to Mademoiselle, Annabelle had green eyes with short prickly lashes that made you think of gooseberries; she was sharp and sour like gooseberries too, and I didn't like her much. Now she went on, baiting Mademoiselle, 'It isn't fair, you know, to be inaccurate. Germans wash and wash, just like Americans—'

'Peegs they are, peegs,' Mademoiselle declared with passion. '*Cochons!* Twice already they have over-run my country since my parents are living!'

Bridget, sitting by my side, nodded consideringly. 'Yes, there is that. All the same, do you think calling the Germans *cochons* is being fair to pigs?'

32

'It's rubbish that pigs are dirty anyway,' I said. 'They're perfectly clean animals so long as the people looking after them muck out their sties properly. Which is a worse job than cowsheds if anyone is asking me—'

'I do not ask you, Peg,' said Mademoiselle, 'and now we will do the *dictée. Prenez les cahiers, s'il vous plait. Ecrivez une lettre. Chère Madame, vergule—*'

'Indigestion again, poor thing,' said Felicity.

Mademoiselle flushed crimson right through her make-up, and I felt sorry for her. I said, 'Shut up, Felicity.'

Mademoiselle paid no attention to either of us. *'Je repète, Chère Madame, vergule—'*

Annabelle said innocently, 'How do you spell *vergule*?'

'This is a *dictée*, Annabelle, and you must not ask how you spell. Besides you know perfectly well it is a comma, *vergule—*'

'It sounds like indigestion to me,' said Felicity. 'Anyway, I shouldn't think the Germans would want to invade us. It's one thing for them to overrun poor old France—'

'What do you mean, Felicity?'

'Well, it's obvious we're better at fighting than the French. Surely you haven't forgotten Waterloo?'

'Ah, *notre cher Napoléon!*' cried Mademoiselle, black eyes on fire, long dark hair tossing. 'Our great he*ro*, the greatest Frenchman we have ever known—' She caught herself, and turned away from Felicity. *'Allons*, the *dictée* once again. *Chère Madame, vergule—'*

'Indigestion,' said Felicity.

The classroom door opened without the usual warning knock and we all scraped to our feet and said in respectful unison, 'Good morning, Miss Miller.'

Miss Miller had worn a blouse of that identical shade of green as long as I could remember. It was always open at the neck; her own neck was red and mottled, like a turkey, and she kept herself straight, shoulders back and head very high. Even a glimpse of her at the far end of the corridor made my mind wriggle uneasily over what I might have done wrong. Had Mademoiselle complained about our behaviour, or one of the other teachers overheard the racket?

Miss Miller closed the door behind her with a click and mounted the two steps to the teacher's desk. 'Good morning, Mademoiselle, good morning girls. Sit down, please.'

She waited for the last scrape of the last chair to end before she went on, smoothly, 'As you know it is not my custom to interrupt a lesson, but today I have something of unusual importance to say to you.'

I wondered if everybody else felt as quaky as I did.

Miss Miller's eyes swept over us all. 'A new girl has joined the school today. She is a little older than you are, but I have decided to place her in this form. Her name is Rosa. I want you to treat her with the greatest possible consideration—' she paused for a moment, '— because, at present, she speaks very little English.'

She paused again, and Felicity put up her hand. 'Please Miss Miller, if she doesn't speak English, what does she speak?'

'She speaks German,' said Miss Miller pleasantly.

Mademoiselle's face went scarlet with indignation and her eyes caught fire once more. 'But it is insupportable, Madame, that I should be required to teach French to a German. And besides it is the order that enemy aliens are interned — I do not at all understand!'

'Rosa is not an enemy alien,' said Miss Miller, her voice like crystals of ice. 'Rosa is a refugee.'

A murmur of surprise and interest rustled round the classroom.

'Even so she is a German —' Mademoiselle protested mutinously, but Miss Miller stopped her short by lifting one hand.

'I'm sure I can count on everybody to be kind to Rosa,' she said blandly, 'and now I shall bring her in and introduce you.'

The silence was complete again, and this time nobody rustled. Miss Miller trod down the two steps in her high

34

heels and opened the door and beckoned, and a small thin dark girl with intense eyes slipped in and stood beside her, hands twisting together.

'This is Rosa,' said Miss Miller. 'Rosa, my dear, here are your new classmates. Mademoiselle will see that you settle in.' She directed a managing smile towards Mademoiselle, nodded and made her exit. Felicity was just too late to open the door for her.

Rosa stood where she was, waiting quietly.

'Now let me see where shall you sit,' said Mademoiselle. Her glance roved round the desks; she avoided looking at Rosa. 'Bridget and Peg, you have always a lot to say — it is better you shall be separated. Bridget must move over beside the window and Rosa shall share with Peg.'

'That's not fair,' complained Bridget. 'Felicity and Annabelle give you lots more trouble than we do.'

But of course, I thought, Mademoiselle was afraid of Felicity and Annabelle.

'No argument, Bridget,' said Mademoiselle. 'Pick up your things and remove.'

The silence came back, as if Miss Miller had left it behind her. Rosa sat down beside me and opened the new exercise book Mademoiselle gave her and uncapped her fountain pen; you could hear the nib scratching as she wrote the date, in English, on the first page.

'Hello,' I whispered.

She nodded back solemnly. After that she kept her eyes down, not looking at any of us though she must have known everyone was looking at her. I wondered what she was thinking. How awful to be in a strange country where nobody spoke your language; where some people, like Mademoiselle, even thought about it as the language of the enemy.

And did Rosa feel like a German, even if she was a refugee? She must have lived in Germany most of her life....

I was glad that I was English — though I had never thought much about it, to tell the truth, until the war made us all so patriotic.

Mademoiselle took advantage of the unusual silence. '*Encore, écrivez. Chère Madame, vergule. . . .*'

Everybody wrote industriously.

When I got home I found to my surprise that Mum had already heard about Rosa in the post office that morning. She knew more about Rosa than I did: Rosa was alone in the world without parents or brothers or sisters, and she was going to live with Mrs Brownrigg.

'I shouldn't think that would be much fun,' I said.

Mrs Brownrigg was rich and stand-offish and she lived by herself, even further from the town than we were, in a big secluded house that was very nearly as grand as the Rutlands'.

'Poor little girl,' sighed Mum.

'She'll find it difficult keeping up at school,' I said. 'She doesn't understand English very well.'

'Then you'll have to help her, Peg,' said Mum.

'*Me?*'

'Oh, not just with schoolwork! With everything. Getting to know people, I mean. Finding a place for herself in the community and feeling as if she belongs.'

It didn't sound my sort of thing at all.

'I don't see what it's got to do with me,' I grumbled. 'Just because Mademoiselle made Rosa sit next to me doesn't mean she's my responsibility—'

'Are you sure?' asked Mum quietly. 'Perhaps it does.'

'That isn't fair—'

'Perhaps it's to do with growing up a little,' said Mum. 'Taking account of what another person needs as well as of what you want yourself. Think about it, Peg.'

'But it sounds terribly complicated and difficult—'

Mum laughed. 'I'm sure you'll find a way,' she said.

'What were you doing in the village at that time, anyway, Mum?' Hazel asked. 'You're usually much too busy to go out halfway through the morning.'

'Well, that's another thing,' said Mum. 'I was collecting our identity cards. People with names beginning with P had to queue up for them at the post office at twelve o'clock.'

She looked in her handbag and brought out four small, squarish, buff-coloured cards, one for each of us.

Except, of course, for Tom. He'd be getting his somewhere else.

I stared down at mine.

'MARGARET VERONICA PRICE. . . .'

How strange. . . .

It gave me an odd, detached feeling; as if I was looking at somebody else's impression of who I was.

'Take care of your cards, now,' Mum said. 'Don't lose them. They're important. By government order every one of us has to carry an identity card everywhere, wherever we go, from now on.'

6

I haven't visited the River Tree since my birthday but now, this evening, I need somewhere quiet and private where I can think.

I need the River Tree.

I climb up into its branches and sit there in my place in its highest fork, and study the small buff-coloured card in my hand.

That's my name written there on it. That's *me*.

MARGARET VERONICA PRICE, DJZJ 69/4.

And I don't recognize myself at all.

Nobody has ever called me Margaret or Veronica, and I've never had a number. Or an 'identity', whatever that may be.

I'm just Peg, part of our family.

Our family is strong, like the chestnut tree. We may argue sometimes, even quarrel, but that doesn't matter; we all know where we are. We have responsibilities to each other *because* we're a family, things we expect and things that are expected of us; Hazel and I have responsibility for the milking. Our family is safe and secure, the castle walls around us. We don't need other people.

But today. . . .

Today Mum told me that perhaps I had responsibility for Rosa. Rosa, who isn't anything to do with our family, who is a stranger, a foreigner. And yet Mum says I have responsibility for her—

Why should that make me feel a little lost, a little afraid?

As if all the things I've taken for granted all my life had shifted ever so slightly underneath me; as if the world is not quite as I have always understood?

The branches of the River Tree stir and its leaves rustle round me in a rushing whisper.

Beyond it, in the distance, the sun is sinking slowly into the horizon.

The light is exactly right.

And suddenly, while I am watching, it happens again. Suddenly the estuary plunders the light from the sun and transfigures it and flings it back against the sky: a pale lemony light now in the last of the sunset, as tangy as if I can taste it on my tongue, and sharp and needle-cold.

A seabird wheels and calls and a shiver of wind skims the river; and from water and wind and light and sky and from the heart of the River Tree itself a question takes wing like the bird and comes to visit me.

A lonely question, a seeking soaring question, a question that only I can ever answer: *if* I ever can.

Who is Peg Price, DJZJ Sixty-nine Four?

Who am I?

7

Autumn slipped into winter, and apart from the blackout and talk of food rationing soon to come, being at war didn't feel very different from the last months of peace. After all the work that had been put in on them, nobody used the trenches or the Andersons, and people began to make jokes about the 'Phoney War,' the 'Sitzkreig'.

Mum didn't joke, though. She said it wasn't anything to joke about, and she wouldn't let Tom come home though many of the other evacuees were returning. When the time came, Mum said, the war would be only too real.

Bridget and Hazel and I tramped home together from school one day and a convoy of lorries drove past us. Three, four, five, six, one after the other; heading for the coast.

The lorries were crammed with soldiers wearing camouflage jackets and tin helmets. They whistled and waved at us, and we waved back.

'Blow us a kiss, girls!' one soldier shouted, and another called out, 'Mind you're waiting for us when we come back.'

'Cheeky things,' Bridget said indignantly.

'The B.E.F.,' said Hazel.

The British Expeditionary Force; the soldiers who were being sent out to France. We heard about them all the time, at school and in the newspapers and on radio programmes like 'Band Waggon'.

Dad had bought a radio at last and now it stood, a shiny brown mahogany box, in a place of honour on the kitchen window sill. We listened to it every evening, especially to the News; at first Shep had barked furiously at the strange voice without a person. Now he'd got used to it and just lay on the rug with one ear cocked back and the whites of his eyes showing.

The convoy of lorries took up our attention so completely that we didn't notice a car slowing beside us until its horn tooted. The driver was in naval uniform. He wore a peaked cap with a gold badge on it, and a single line of gold braid zigzagged across the cuff of each sleeve.

'Stephen!' I screamed.

'Jump in,' he said, laughing as he leaned across to open the doors. 'Meet Sub-Lieutenant Rutland, RNVR.'

'Oh Stephen, you look wonderful!' I said. 'And what does it mean, RNVR?'

'The Royal Naval Volunteer Reserve,' he said, and tapped the braid. 'They call us the Wavy Navy.' But he wasn't looking at me, he was looking at Hazel. And not in his old way, either. Differently; as if something had happened to her — or to him? — that changed the way he saw her.

'Small fry in the back,' he said. 'Hazel in front.'

I hopped in behind him and Bridget followed. Then Hazel slid in at his side, blushing just enough to give her eyes a sparkle and her cheeks a delicate bloom; I could see it from where I sat.

Stephen said, still looking at her, 'It was nice of you to write.'

'You didn't answer my letter.'

'No. I'm rotten at writing letters. I came, instead. As soon as I could get leave. . . .'

They sat there smiling at each other as if Bridget and I didn't exist, and with the engine purring away wasting petrol.

'Did you miss me, then?' asked Stephen.

'Of course,' I said truthfully, but he wasn't listening.

'Certainly not!' said Hazel, and laughed.

Bridget didn't say a single word.

Stephen dropped Bridget off on the way and then drove us home, and when Mum and Dad saw the car in the yard, and then Stephen in his naval uniform, they both came out to congratulate him. Dad shook Stephen's hand in both his own, and Mum kissed him and asked him to stay for supper.

We sat listening at the table while he told us about his training and the things he'd been doing all these weeks. I could hardly eat for listening, and I fell in love with him all over again.

But he didn't see me at all.

'A destroyer,' Hazel said. 'Can't you even tell us its name?'

'No,' said Stephen. 'Careless talk.'

CARELESS TALK COSTS LIVES, I thought; just like the posters said. Even knowing a ship's name or where it was at any time might cost the lives of the crew, if the information got into the wrong hands. And you never knew who might be a spy. . . .

'Henry is on a cruiser,' I said. 'He's a gunner.'

'When do you have to report back, Stephen?' asked Mum.

'On Saturday.'

'So soon—?'

'Yes. I've only got a forty-eight hour leave.'

Stephen's eyes went back to Hazel's again, locking into them in a way that closed the two of them off from the rest of us. His smile for her was warm and yet oddly diffident, as if he wasn't entirely sure of himself. *Stephen*, not sure of himself—

'Then where will you be going?' Hazel asked.

'I'm not allowed to say.'

'Be like Dad, keep Mum,' I quoted from the posters and giggled.

'As long as it makes you safer I don't mind not knowing,' said Hazel.

'As a matter of fact,' said Stephen, 'I don't even know myself.'

'Security,' said Dad, and nodded in satisfaction.

Stephen polished off the final crusty piece of apple pie and the last scrape of cream. 'That was a super meal, Mrs Price,' he said. 'I'll think about it when I'm tossing on distant oceans.' He turned to my sister. 'What about coming for a drive, Hazel, while I've got my father's car?'

Mum said quickly, 'Yes, why don't you, dear? Peg and I will do the washing up.'

Happiness leaped in Hazel's face. 'All right,' she said, and went to get her coat.

'Take a torch,' advised Dad. 'And mind the blackout when you open the door.'

Hazel and Stephen went out together. I watched them go. They walked out of the house side by side, their hands not touching.

'Such a fine young man,' said Mum later. She ran hot water over a soapy plate and stacked it against the others on the draining board. 'Joining the Navy as soon as war was declared, not even waiting for his call-up—'

'Yes,' I said glumly. My dish-towel was sopping. I dug another one out of the drawer.

Mum handed me a cup to dry. 'Come on, slowcoach, I haven't anywhere to put this. . . . And when he was doing so well at Cambridge, too.' She sighed.

'What about Stephen's exams?' I asked. 'You always say they're so important—'

Only last July she and Dad had been coaxing Hazel to stay on at school for another year, even though she didn't want to. Coaxing — badgering, I'd say; in the end Hazel had given in.

'It's different now,' said Mum. 'There's a war on.'

I lay hunched up under the bedclothes, waiting for Hazel to come in and thinking of all the things that were different because there was a war on.

Tom far away, the blackout, the ARP, Henry and Stephen in the Navy; extra work, sandbags round the school.

(School: Rosa. And for some reason, Rosa was on my conscience.)

And now, Stephen and Hazel, together; the war had done that too. The tears I'd been holding back all evening began to run.

I tried to imagine what it would have been like if he'd asked me to come for a drive instead of Hazel. But somehow, I couldn't imagine it at all. Whenever I tried to think up a conversation between us my mind went blank.

It *would* be Hazel he'd noticed first, of course. She was nearly eighteen now, and so pretty. . . . And *nice*.

I wasn't either.

Dependable, capable, perhaps. It was me, after all, who had been asked to crew Stephen's boat and look after Rosa; I wasn't bad at everyday unromantic things like that. And some people — Dan for instance, or Tom — might think I was fun to be with.

But I wasn't pretty like Hazel, and I wasn't nice.

Now my hanky was nearly as sopping as the dish towel. I screwed it up disgustedly into a ball and hurled it across the room. Tears made you feel worse, not better. They hadn't shifted the solid block of salt in the middle of my throat one inch, and if I didn't stop now I'd look a mess tomorrow, blotched and swollen; everyone would know I'd been crying. I used up some furious energy punching my pillow into the shape I wanted it and lay straight out, on my stomach.

Hazel came in at last and tiptoed over to my bed without putting on the light.

'Peg, are you awake? I've got so much to tell you. Peg, *Stephen kissed me—*'

I lay quite still, one arm shielding my half-turned face. Hazel and I had shared secrets ever since we were tiny — but this time, I didn't want to know.

After a moment she added softly, 'He asked me to be his girlfriend. Oh Peg, I'm so *happy* —' She sounded as if she couldn't quite believe it herself.

Still I didn't answer. She sighed, and I knew I'd hurt her, blunted, just a little, the bright edge of her happiness. But I couldn't help it. I couldn't lie there and listen to her telling about herself and Stephen and it wasn't fair of her to expect me to.

I heard her padding quietly across the carpet in her slippers, and then the curtain rings rattled on the wooden bar as she drew aside the blackout. From under my arm I risked a peep at her. She was sitting with her elbows propped on the sill and her chin on her clasped hands, gazing out at the stars that winked and glittered in the still, dark sky.

Part of me longed to jump out of bed and run over and hug her and say, 'Tell me all about it. Everything he said, everything you said. Share it with me. . . .'

Only I couldn't. *I'd* wanted to be the one Stephen kissed, *I'd* dreamed of being his girl—

A tiny doubt wriggled suddenly in my mind. *Was* that what I wanted — really? Stephen was so much older than me, three whole years; I wasn't quite sure I could have coped.

But of course that was nonsense, I'd always loved Stephen.

And now he was Hazel's boyfriend, and I was left out in the cold.

The tears squeezed out again, scalding against my eyelids. Nobody who was nice could hate her sister.

Annabelle leaned against the classroom door, folding her arms and crossing one ankle over the other.

'All right,' she said tauntingly. 'Tell us what happened to you, then. That is if you really are a refugee!'

Rosa's thin, sallow face went even paler. She said, 'Please, to let me pass.'

'Not until we've heard your story,' said Annabelle.

It was half past three and Mademoiselle had rushed off the instant the bell rang, leaving us to clear up before we went home. That was just like Mademoiselle, of course. Most other teachers would have seen us out before they left, but Mademoiselle had such a miserable time with our class that she couldn't escape fast enough once the lesson was over.

'There is no story,' said Rosa. 'I am here, that is enough.'

'Leave her alone, Annabelle,' I protested. 'You're always picking on Rosa!'

'Because she's a German,' said Annabelle. 'A horrible Hun.'

45

I said disgustedly, 'You might as well pick on somebody because they happen to have blue eyes. Like Felicity —'

But Annabelle wasn't listening to me. 'Go on, Rosa,' she taunted. 'Deny it!'

Rosa couldn't deny it, of course. She just stood there, tiny and somehow withdrawn, staring back at Annabelle out of great dark eyes that looked too big for her face.

'There you are,' said Annabelle. 'She is a German.'

'What if she is?' I demanded. 'It isn't her fault. Nobody chooses what country they're born in.' I was always in a hurry to get home after school, there were so many chores waiting to be done.

'*What if she is?*' repeated Annabelle, as if she couldn't believe she'd heard right. 'I should think you'd know by this time that we're at war, Peg Price.'

'Oh come on, Annabelle,' said Bridget. I was pleased Bridget had come into the argument on my side. She'd been strange and distant all day, oddly quiet; come to think of it, she hadn't been her usual happy-go-lucky self for some time. But now she said staunchly, 'It's perfectly obvious Rosa hasn't got anything to do with the war.'

'Don't you be too sure of that,' said Felicity.

The other girls had gathered around us now. The trouble was, I thought guiltily, Rosa hadn't made friends with anyone. Rosa kept herself to herself. Had we left her out of things because she was a German?

Surely not. I could remember at least once when I'd asked her to join a game of Monopoly at lunch time, and she'd said she had to study, as if she really preferred to be alone.

Now Annabelle said, 'What does she do all by herself every day after school?'

'She goes home to Mrs Brownrigg, of course,' said Bridget.

'Yes, indeed. . . .' Annabelle's gooseberry eyes narrowed to green slits as she added, 'And nobody knows much about *her*, either.'

'Yes we do. We know she's a widow and she lives in that

big house off the Dover road—' I began, and then stopped. That was all I did know.

'And she's rich and eccentric,' said Felicity. 'And goes on holiday to Germany. Or at least she did, until the war.'

'She is very kind to me,' said Rosa, her voice shaking. 'Kinder than any of you—'

'Of *course* she is!' said Annabelle. 'Refugee, indeed! Shall I tell you what I think?'

'You may tell what you like,' said Rosa. 'You do not know.'

'What I think,' said Annabelle, 'is that both of them, Mrs Brownrigg and Rosa, are spying. *From their house that's on the Dover road*, just like Peg said!'

'Spying?' said Bridget incredulously. '*Rosa*? That's rubbish—'

Rosa had gone completely white. 'It's not true. Not true.'

'Just like the posters,' said Annabelle, nodding triumphantly. 'Careless talk.' Rosa listens to what people say and tells Mrs Brownrigg, and they pass messages back to Germany, in German—'

'Nonsense!' I shouted. 'That's ridiculous!'

'No it isn't,' said Annabelle. 'Felicity heard them talking German together in the butcher's. That's proof.'

'No — ' said Rosa.

'Then you give *us* proof,' said Annabelle. 'Tell us everything that happened to you in Germany. *Prove* that you're a refugee.'

Rosa doubled up suddenly with her arms pressing into her stomach as if she had a terrible pain. I said, 'Sit down,' and helped her into the nearest desk. She looked as if she might faint.

Then I turned on the whole pack of them and lost my temper. 'Get out!' I told them. 'Annabelle, Felicity, all of you, get *out*! The only one here with any decency at all is Bridget. The rest of you get right out of here and *leave us alone*!'

Annabelle uncrossed her arms and came away from the door. She looked scared; perhaps she was afraid she'd gone too far. She said sulkily, 'Well, if you and Bridget want to be on Rosa's side —'

'We do,' said Bridget.

'It was only a bit of fun,' said Felicity. 'We didn't mean anything.'

'All she had to do was tell about being a refugee,' said Annabelle. 'You'd think she'd want to tell if it was exciting —'

'Just leave us alone,' I said.

Everybody began to talk at once, pretending nothing had happened. They hurried out of the room in twos and threes, Annabelle and Felicity first.

Rosa straightened up slowly. She looked from me to Bridget and then back to me. Her eyes were dry and tragic. 'Now you have quarrelled with your friends, and it is over me. . . .'

'They're not our friends,' I said stormily. 'They're stupid and mean and I hate them. I don't want friends like that.'

'They're not so bad really,' said Bridget. 'It just got out of hand.'

'It is when things get out of hand that people are hurt,' Rosa said. 'One day I will tell you what happened. . . .' Her teeth began to chatter; she was shivering.

'Are you all right?' I asked.

'Yes, all right. It is just that I cannot speak — I do not want to speak — about any of it — not yet.'

'We don't want to know,' I said. 'Not until you want to tell us. Come on, let's walk home together.'

8

By the time we reached the school gates it was four o'clock
and Hazel had already gone.

I knew why she hadn't waited, of course. She wanted to
get all her jobs done as fast as possible so that she'd have
more time with Stephen if he came round again tonight.

I'd been horribly conscious, walking to school with
Hazel that morning, of the strain between us. Not the usual
after-a-squabble crossness that blows away as soon as one
of you relents and says 'Sorry!' This was different. It
frightened me.

Earlier, her mind hadn't been on a single thing she was
doing. She'd clipped the milking cups on to the same cow's
udder twice, and she emptied a whole bucketful of milk
down the dairy sluice instead of into the cooler. Any other
time Mum would have been furious, but today all she did
was laugh and say, 'You must be in love.' Personally I
thought that was a completely irritating excuse. I couldn't
see why being in love was any reason to act as if you were
halfwitted.

Hazel had not tried a second time to confide in me. In a
way I didn't blame her — I couldn't even be sure she realized
how miserable I was. She seemed to be walking in a
different world, a world that had no room for me.

I could have borne not getting Stephen, it wasn't that; I'd
never *really* expected him to notice me. *But Hazel getting
him instead* — that was what tied my stomach in knots.
Every time I remembered about them, all day long, a savage
angry resentment had gnawed away at me, burning and
stinging me deep inside.

But now for a little while Rosa's troubles had pushed
mine into the background.

She said now, 'It is kind of you, Bridget and Peg, to let me
walk home with you.'

'Come with us every day.' Such an easy thing to say, why

49

hadn't I said it before?

A few of the other girls were standing outside the corner shop swopping sweets. They nodded as we went past, looking embarrassed, but they didn't speak.

'They do not like me,' said Rosa.

'Nonsense!' I said. 'Anyway, that's only Annabelle's crowd — you don't want to bother about them. We like you — don't we, Bridget?'

'Of course,' said Bridget.

If only Rosa wasn't so quiet, always retiring into herself, I thought irritably; if only she'd join in more, be more fun—

'Look,' I said, plunging in with both feet before I had time to think about it, 'the thing is, Rosa, you don't *try* to make people like you. You have to make a bit of effort yourself!'

She looked at me out of her big dark eyes. I wondered why I'd started this. Well, I had; now I'd have to go on. There must be *some* way to make her more popular.

'What we need,' I said, thinking aloud, 'is something you're really good at, Rosa. Something different from the rest of us.'

Then, I thought, she'd still stand out from the crowd but it would be the right kind of standing out, the kind to make people admire her.

'Isn't there anything special you can do?'

Rosa stopped suddenly and for a moment I thought she really was going to come up with a hidden talent, perhaps even something spectacular. Then she shook her head and her eyes dropped. 'No. There is nothing.'

'Well, can you sing?'

'No.'

'Or act?'

There were still six weeks to go before school closed for Christmas. Perhaps we could organize a pantomime — yes, that was brilliant! True, some of the others were quite good at acting, but with a bit of luck Rosa might outshine them.

'No,' said Rosa. 'At acting I am no good.'

'Games then? Hockey?' But I knew that was hopeless even while I was suggesting it. Rosa simply tagged along yards behind everyone else on the hockey pitch, trailing her stick and looking bored and frozen.

'Conjuring? Card tricks?'

She didn't even understand what I meant.

'*You* think of something,' I prodded Bridget. It struck me Bridget wasn't being much help.

'Only one thing there is I am good at,' said Rosa. 'German!'

Well, at least she'd made a joke.

'Your English is getting better every day,' I said encouragingly.

She smiled and shook her head, and then sighed. 'I do not blame them, those girls. The black sheep I am. And the black sheep is not well come in.'

'Black sheep—?'

'I am different, that is the trouble. In wartime to be different, it is not forgivable. I know.'

'There's nothing wrong with being different,' I began, and then Bridget stopped short on the road and said with sudden, astonishing violence, 'That's where you're wrong — there *is*! Being different is *terrible*. You don't understand, Peg — nobody understands!'

Bridget wasn't talking about Rosa, I thought, she was talking about *herself*. Otherwise she wouldn't have sounded so vehement, her eyes wouldn't have looked so stormy. But how could Bridget — ordinary cheerful uncomplicated Bridget who'd been my best friend as long as I could remember — how could *Bridget* be 'different'?

I stood there staring at her. Her face was flushed and she was nearly crying, but there was something more. She was angry too; bitterly, deeply angry.

I said, 'Bridget, whatever's the matter?'

'Nothing. *Nothing* — leave me alone!' She jerked her eyes away from me down the road ahead, and I saw her stiffen suddenly. The flush died out of her cheeks, leaving them pale. 'Look,' she said. 'Leonard.'

Somebody was riding towards us on a bicycle, somebody in RAF uniform. She was right, of course.

I said, 'Hullo, Leonard! Goodness, you look well.'

He did, almost as handsome as Stephen. The uniform suited him. His hair was slicked back under the perky little blue cap; he seemed taller, older, much more interesting.

'So the girls all tell me,' he said, laughing, 'but thanks anyway. Who's your new friend?'

'Rosa,' I said, without going into complicated explanations. 'I didn't know you'd joined up!'

'I knew,' said Bridget.

'Three weeks ago, to be exact. I couldn't let them win the war without me — and, to show their appreciation, they've given me a long weekend already.'

'Oh,' I said. 'Stephen's home too, have you seen him?'

'Not yet.'

'Everybody seems to be joining up,' I said desolately.

'Not *quite* everybody,' said Leonard. His eyebrows tilted up in that odd way of his and the whites of his eyes gleamed as he looked at Bridget and laughed softly. 'Ah well, mustn't stop now. Be seeing you!'

Bridget stood watching as he pedalled away, the colour surging back into her face again.

'Oh dear,' I said in dismay. 'Bridget, surely you haven't gone overboard about Leonard, have you? I mean, Leonard—'

She went on looking after him without answering, and suddenly I felt awkward. There was I, rushing in tactlessly. . . . Even if I didn't like Leonard much, he was in the RAF serving his country. And Bridget had a right to take a fancy for anyone she chose.

'Sorry,' I mumbled. 'I didn't mean that, it was stupid. Leonard's all right.'

'Peg—'

Bridget was on the brink of telling me something, I was sure of that.

'Yes?' I said quickly.

Then she changed her mind.

'Nothing,' she said, and shook her head impatiently. 'Come on, let's get home. We're late.'

We reached Bridget's house first and then, five minutes later, the gate to our farm. Rosa went on towards Mrs Brownrigg's, further down the Dover road, and turned in between the ploughed winter fields. One day soon, perhaps, I'd invite Rosa home with me, but not today.

I dragged myself along, my head aching and my legs weighted with tiredness. Everything was going wrong, I thought. Stephen and Hazel, Rosa, now even Bridget. . . . And me. I couldn't remember ever feeling so mixed up and unhappy in my life before.

Mum was putting away the ironing board as I came into the kitchen. There was a smell of gingerbread, fresh and spicy.

She said, 'Oh, thank goodness, Peg, you're home at last. Put those sheets away in the airing cupboard for me, will you? And then if you'd run over to the dairy, while you've got your coat on, and bring some butter—'

'Where's Hazel?' I asked.

'She's gone out with Stephen in the car. And Peg, some eggs too, while you're at it. I don't seem to have had a minute all day.'

I put away the sheets, fetched the butter and the eggs and took off my coat, while Mum poured us each a cup of tea, steaming hot, and cut two thick slices off the gingerbread. Then she pulled a couple of chairs up to the kitchen range.

'Come and toast yourself, you look frozen.' Two small worry lines deepened between her eyebrows. 'In fact, Peg, you're looking a bit peaky altogether. Are you feeling all right?'

'Yes, of course,' I said.

'Sure?' She sighed. 'Perhaps we're letting you work too hard, with all the extra jobs you've been doing at home lately on top of school.'

'Honestly, I'm fine.'

'Then did anything go wrong at school today?' Mum asked.

'Well. . . .'

All of a sudden I wanted desperately to tell her about my

troubles. When I was little she'd always been able to put things right for me; perhaps she could now. Perhaps she'd know how to help Rosa fit in with the crowd, perhaps she'd know what was the matter with Bridget. Perhaps she'd even know how I could sort myself out over Hazel and Stephen.

My words rushed tumbling out of me.

'Oh, Mum. Everything's horrible lately! There's Annabelle. She's always picking on Rosa — some of the others do it too. They seem to hate her!'

'Hate Rosa?' Mum looked astonished. 'But why?'

'Just because she's German.'

'Oh dear,' Mum said. 'That's what war does, of course. It makes people so narrow minded and prejudiced—'

'Prejudiced?'

'Yes — they make up their minds about other people because of something like being German, without waiting to find out what they're really like, as people. Without trying to understand. I suppose in wartime it's bound to happen, but still. . . .'

'It isn't fair to hate a person because of something they can't help!'

'No,' said Mum. 'It isn't fair. In fact, it's *wrong*. Besides, there are always two sides to every argument, two points of view. Try to remember that, Peg.'

Then the telephone started ringing.

'Just a minute, dear,' Mum said, and went to answer it.

By the time she came back her tea was cold and she herself was in a fuss.

'Peg, do you think you could make supper for yourself and Dad tonight? I simply haven't got time, I'll have to rush —'

'All right,' I said.

'That was Mrs Harrison on the phone. She's gone down with shingles and she's asked me to take her place tonight — it's the Red Cross. There's a lady from the St John Ambulance in London coming to lecture us on shock treatment and I've promised to meet her train. Peg, I'm sorry—'

'It doesn't matter.'

'Shingles can be dreadfully painful, Aunt Prue had them right across her chest. Poor Mrs Harrison. . . . Oh, Peg! I've got to chair the meeting too, and introduce this Mrs. . . . Mrs. . . .' She stopped, panic in her face. 'Now I can't even remember her name—'

'Ring Mrs Harrison back and ask,' I suggested.

'Yes, of course. Of course.'

It was funny, I thought, how Mum could cope with all sorts of things, the farm and the house and the family, and be completely calm and capable, and yet fly into a total flap because she had to meet somebody she didn't know off a train.

'Don't worry,' I said. 'You'll be great at chairing the meeting, and at introducing Mrs Whoeversheis and everything else. And Dad and I will be fine. I'll just heat up the rest of that soup from last night and scramble some eggs, and there's the gingerbread too.'

'Oh Peg, you're always so practical. I don't know how we'd manage without you!' She laughed suddenly, and pinched my cheek. 'And here am I landing you with *my* work just when I was saying you look tired!'

It wasn't being tired I minded, only that for once I really had wanted to talk to her.

There was no chance of that now. She went off to phone Mrs Harrison and change. Ten minutes later she came down again looking trim and pretty in her navy blue suit, and then she'd gone.

Dad gave me a hand with the milking and after that we fed the calves and the chickens, and then we noticed that Shep was limping. I held him while Dad probed about until he got a thorn out of his paw. Shep growled a bit while Dad was doing it but afterwards he licked my face, and Dad said he wouldn't have kept as still as that for anyone but me.

I liked working with Dad, just the two of us together. It made me feel responsible.

Later on he offered to stir the soup while I cooked the

eggs, and we ate our supper beside the fire. I began to wonder if perhaps I might be able to talk to Dad; really talk, about things that mattered.

After a while, when we'd finished eating, I said cautiously, 'Dad?'

'Well, Peg?'

'Suppose . . . suppose somebody's done something you feel awful, really terrible about.'

'Terrible?'

It wasn't easy to pick the right word. I wanted to keep it vague, at least to begin with. Perhaps later we'd come down to names, to what had actually happened. 'Yes, terrible,' I said. 'Angry and miserable both together — even if you know it isn't really their fault and it's something you might have done yourself if you got the chance, only you never would and they did—'

Dad began to light his pipe, drawing on it, giving it a lot of attention.

'And at the same time,' I went on after a moment, 'even while you hate them, you know you do actually love them quite a lot.' (Would he recognize Hazel from that? Did I want him to?) 'Well,' I said, hunching up in my chair and almost wishing I hadn't started any of this, 'how can you sort things out?'

Dad puffed quietly, blowing small clouds of bluish smoke. Then he said, 'Well,' and cleared his throat. 'Well—'

I waited.

'Hard to know,' he said. 'Now if you were asking me something practical, Peg, like how to mend a puncture. . . .'

I wasn't. He'd taught me that already, and other things too, useful things; how to change a fuse, how to build a haystack, how to unblock the sink last winter when Mum had the flu and it was jammed with grease and tea-leaves.

'People are more difficult,' I said.

The clock on the sideboard struck ten.

'Goodness,' said Dad. 'That time already? I'll have to get busy on those accounts for the bank manager.'

I went up to bed on my own for the second night running. If I could fall asleep before Hazel came in, I thought, I wouldn't have to talk to her.

But somehow sleep didn't arrive.

Instead, all the day's problems thrashed and twisted in my mind, dragging at me and tangling together. Faces; voices. Hazel, Stephen, myself; Rosa and Bridget and me. And Mum and then Dad, both busy, both taken up with worries of their own and with no time to listen to mine.

And yet . . . Echoing through, tapping away at the corner of my mind, I found the one word they both had used: *practical.*

Perhaps if I could find one practical thing to do. . . .

I switched on the bedside light and sat up, pulling the eiderdown round my shoulders to ward off the chilliness of the room. One practical thing —

Not about Hazel and Stephen, I thought. That was beyond me, just as it had been beyond me to prevent Tom being sent away. And Bridget; at present, I didn't even know what was the matter with her. But because I couldn't do everything, it didn't mean I couldn't do *anything.*

Rosa. Rosa had said she couldn't act. But perhaps if we put on a pantomime she could get involved in some other way; in the chorus perhaps, dancing, or helping with stage decorations or lighting. At any rate, I'd make sure she was one of the crowd instead of always being the odd one out.

That was it! A pantomime!

Suddenly I found excitement and anticipation running through me like an ocean tide, sweeping away the unhappiness that had weighed me down all day, all through the last twenty-four hours. I was alive and energetic again, ready to go.

I switched off the light and lay down. Tomorrow I'd go and talk to the River Tree.

I'm finding out about Peg Price, I'd say. She isn't pretty, like Hazel, and she can be jealous. And jealousy is a bitter, corroding acid; it dissolves her self-respect.

But there are good things about her too. Today Peg Price

stood up for a person the others were ganging up on, and even though it was uncomfortable it felt right.

And she is *practical.*

9

We started on the pantomime immediately. I found there was no problem getting the rest of the class interested. School had begun to drag in recent weeks, with even the air raid practices becoming routine, and the idea of putting on a pantomime caught everyone's enthusiasm. We settled on 'Aladdin', and soon there was so much to do, and so little time to do it in if the show was going to be ready for January, that everything else took second place. In fact Stephen going back to his ship was almost made up for, as far as I was concerned, by Hazel taking her fair share of the farmwork once again.

And just as I was discovering the problems of trying to organize an assortment of people who all have different opinions about how things ought to be done, Mr Gill offered to help.

Mr Gill taught English and he was middle-aged and forceful; it was a relief to hand over the whole business of casting and production to him. Then Mrs Pinckney, who was our own English teacher, let it slip that she'd once been a ballet dancer and knew a little about choreography. That turned out to be an understatement — she was wonderful at it, and from that point onwards the pantomime took off.

Annabelle was to be Aladdin, Mr Gill decided after several auditions; Bridget was the Sultan, and I was the Genie of the Lamp. And there was no doubt at all who would play the Princess: Felicity. She had the exact kind of long, fairytale golden hair that would cast her automatically for the part and even at that stage it was clear she was the best actress in the class. I might have guessed, I thought crossly, that it was Felicity and not Rosa who would stand out from the crowd.

Rosa, and everyone else who hadn't been given a speaking part, was in the chorus. I had to be content with that.

Mrs Pinckney took care to see that Rosa understood her directions, but she needn't have worried. Rosa seemed to know what to do by instinct.

I stood behind Mrs Pinckney in the wings watching the chorus rehearse their opening sequence for the first time on the school stage, and hugged myself. Rosa didn't stand out from everyone else in the way I'd hoped, but it didn't matter. Something even better was happening: she fitted in, she was one of the crowd.

Mrs Pinckney seemed to pick up my thoughts. 'That little German girl is doing quite well. . . .' Then she sighed. 'Poor child. After everything she's suffered —'

'What?' I said.

Mrs Pinckney jumped. 'Oh, Peg — I didn't notice you there! Where has Mr Gill got to?'

Mr Gill came fussing up from backstage, scratching at his bristly chin with one hand and flapping the sheets of script in the other. 'All right, that'll do for the chorus. Let them go home and we'll run through the second scene again with the principals. I'm not happy about it, not happy at all. . . .'

Mrs Pinckney dismissed the dancers, complimenting them on working so hard. Frankly I thought that had a lot to do with Mrs Pinckney herself; she was the sort of person who made you *want* to do your best.

'Now you lot,' said Mr Gill, flapping his sheets at us again. 'Sultan, Aladdin, Genie, Princess. . . . Here we are half way through December and we haven't got it right yet. Could you all manage tomorrow morning, even though it's Saturday? We've got to make some progress before we break up for Christmas. I'm not at all happy about the Dame—'

He'd cast Nan Webster as the Dame, but only, as he'd made it clear at the time, with a question mark. And since then he'd rewritten the script and given the Dame twice as much to do.

'We really can't put on a proper pantomime without a proper Dame,' he grumbled now. His eyes looked bleared as well as gloomy, as if he hadn't found time to go to bed. 'It ought to be somebody hefty with hairy legs. Mr Jones would have been ideal for it if he hadn't gone and joined up.'

'We could pad Nan out a bit here and there,' suggested Mrs Pinckney.

Nan looked furious. She was plump enough already.

'No no no no,' said Mr Gill testily. 'It's the *legs* that matter. A pantomime is a traditional entertainment and it's completely pointless unless you do it in the traditional way. The Dame has to lift up his skirt and cavort about and be aggressively masculine—' He ran a hand through his hair, irritated and impatient. 'For goodness' sake, there must be somebody left who isn't in the Services!'

I said, 'Well, there is—'

He whisked round on me. 'Yes, yes, who?'

No doubt Dan too, like all the other boys, would soon be in uniform but for the moment I happened to know he was free, without even a job; I'd run into him in the town last Saturday. We'd hardly seen anything of him since the war started and, now I thought about it, I'd missed him. It would be good to have him around. And surely if Mr Gill was as intent as all that on a masculine Dame, he wouldn't object to casting somebody outside the school.

'Bridget's brother,' I said hopefully. 'Dan.'

'Do you think he'd be willing?' barked Mr Gill and whisked round again, this time on Bridget.

Bridget stared back at him, her face sulky and scarlet. What *was* wrong with her these days? The old Bridget wouldn't have hesitated.

'Dan's always ready for anything,' I said, as she didn't answer. 'Of course he'll do it!'

In any case, Mr Gill wasn't going to consider refusal. 'Let me see,' he said, fingers combing through his hair again, contemplatively now. 'We'll put the show on in mid-January, so you could tell him it'll mean rehearsals two or three times a week, Bridget, excluding Christmas. . . . Could you bring him along tomorrow morning?'

'All right!' said Bridget. Unaccountably, she sounded almost defiant. 'I'll ask him!'

61

'Excellent,' said Mr Gill. 'Now, Aladdin and the Princess centre stage, please. And the rest of you out of sight so Mrs Pinckney and I can concentrate.'

We backed away and the rehearsal began again, Annabelle still a bit stiff as Aladdin, and Felicity trilling off her lines as if she'd been born a Princess. Even Mr Gill couldn't fault Felicity's acting, I thought, whatever problems he might have with the rest of us.

Bridget squatted on her heels in a corner of the wings, and I slipped in beside her. She still had that odd, shut-down look about her, as if she was trying to fend people off — even me.

'What's wrong?' I whispered.

'Nothing,' she said. 'I've got to go over my part.'

'But there isn't enough light here to read —'

'In my head,' said Bridget.

The rest of the rehearsal ran through without too much difficulty; of course we'd have to put in some intensive polishing tomorrow morning, said Mr Gill, rubbing his bristles again. On the whole, though, it was going well. Only Nan looked disconsolate.

'We'll have to find another part for Nan,' Mrs Pinckney decided as we were about to dismiss. 'You really can't cast someone as a principal and then leave her out altogether, it isn't fair. I know, she can be Buttons.'

'I thought Buttons was in Cinderella,' protested Annabelle.

'I'm sure Mr Gill can write a Buttons into Aladdin,' said Mrs Pinckney. Her eyes twinkled at me across the stage. 'After all, he managed to cast the Genie exactly right, didn't he? It isn't everybody who can conjure up a masculine Dame just when we need one!'

When I reached home, rather late, Mum wasn't there. She had decided quite suddenly, soon after we left for school, to go and see Tom, and she'd packed a bag and caught the next train.

'You can see why, of course,' said Hazel. 'Christmas.'

I knew what she meant. Mum had made the cake yesterday and for a few hours the house had felt like Christmas already, with frost glittering the window panes and spicy smells filling the air. Any other year I'd have been deep in preparations myself by now, buying and making presents, wrapping them up, hiding them away so that nobody could guess by the size or shape what I was going to give them. This year, I hadn't even started. I couldn't bear to think about Christmas without Tom.

Now it struck me that because Tom wasn't here what we all needed was to put *more* effort into Christmas, not less; more than ever before, to cheer things up.

'Why don't you and I make the mince pies tonight and surprise Mum when she gets home?' I suggested. 'Forget about homework. Some things are more important.'

Hazel's face lit up. She hadn't looked like that since Stephen went away again. 'Oh Peg, yes, let's. It won't take long if we do it together.'

She didn't add, 'and it'll be like old times,' but I knew that was what she was thinking. I couldn't reach out to meet her though, not any further than I'd gone already. The pantomime might have taken my mind off Hazel and Stephen temporarily, but nothing had changed; whenever I thought about them the hurt was still there, raging and raw inside me.

But for this evening I wouldn't think about them at all, I'd think about Christmas, and mince pies.

I rubbed and kneaded and rolled, getting flour up to my elbows and all over my skirt, and Hazel greased patty tins and cut rounds of pastry and filled them with mincemeat and then sprinkled the tops with sugar. The clock's hands swung round with unbelievable speed. It seemed no time till the pies were in the oven and Dad came in for a late snack before bed. He looked tired, sitting there by the big black-leaded range where the pies were baking, sipping cocoa.

Hazel said, 'Dad, you're working too hard.'

He nodded, not arguing about it.

'You wouldn't think one man could make all that

63

difference,' I said. 'Henry must have done an awful lot of things round here.'

Dad laughed. 'Well, yes. He did.'

'Couldn't you get someone else?' asked Hazel.

'It isn't so easy,' said Dad. 'All the fit young men are going into the Services. Perhaps one of these days I'll find somebody — but whoever it is, he won't be Henry.'

Afterwards I thought how strange it was that Dad should have used those words. At the time, though, I hardly noticed.

'Nothing from Stephen?' Dad was asking Hazel. 'No letter?'

'Nothing,' said Hazel.

So perhaps Stephen wasn't all that struck on her after all, I thought swiftly. If he wasn't writing. . . .

'He'll be all right,' Dad said.

'Yes,' said Hazel. 'I don't mind, just as long as he's safe. That's all that matters—'

'He'll be at sea,' Dad said gently. 'Nothing to get anxious over, chicken. You'd have heard if anything was wrong.'

'Yes,' said Hazel again. She turned her head away, and in spite of everything I felt almost sorry for her; I hadn't realized she would worry quite so much over Stephen's safety. Over other girls, now — that's what I would have worried about, in her place.

'You could go and see Dr Rutland, of course,' Dad said. 'Or Stephen's mother. That would set your mind at rest—'

Hazel looked horrified. 'Dr Rutland. I wouldn't *dare*—'

I didn't blame her. The Rutlands simply were not the sort of people we went to see, not without an invitation. And that would only happen in very special circumstances, like the beginning of the war.

Shep got up suddenly from where he was lying under the table and began to bark, short loud excited barks, his head cocked and his tail wagging frantically as he scratched at the door to get out.

'Surely not Mum already?' Hazel questioned. 'But she was going to stay the night, at least.'

'It's a car, anyway,' said Dad.

We peered past the edge of the blackout curtains. A taxi had stopped at the yard entrance, its headlamps, partly covered with brown paper, showing barely enough light to drive by. We could see Mum paying the driver. And behind her there was someone else, someone I could only just make out in the darkness.

'*Tom*!' I screamed, and forgot the blackout altogether as Shep and I both raced, scrambling and tripping over each other, out of the back door to reach him.

Tom; after all these weeks and months, *Tom*. I couldn't believe it. I hugged him. He smelt of chips and vinegar and warm little boy, and he hugged me back so hard that it hurt.

Then the taxi drove away and we all went inside into the kitchen again, and Tom sat on the floor with both his arms round Shep's neck.

'I couldn't help it, Richard,' Mum said after the fuss had died down a bit. She sounded defensive, as if she'd done something wrong. 'As soon as I saw him, I knew I couldn't walk away and leave him behind.'

'What about bombs?' asked Dad.

'There haven't been any.'

'Not so far—'

'It's more important to be together,' said Mum. She was pale. 'Especially now.'

Suddenly it was very quiet. 'What does that mean?' asked Dad.

She said with painful slowness, 'I heard it at the station this morning. From the ticket inspector. He told me. . . .'

She stopped. She was shaking.

'Go on,' Dad's voice said into the quietness. 'He told you what?'

'Henry's been killed,' said Mum.

10

I'd never before known anyone who died, and to me the strangest part of it, the thought that haunted me, was the way that nothing else stopped, nothing else at all, only Henry.

Everything else went on. Ten o'clock, eleven o'clock, midnight, morning; Saturday, Sunday, next week, next month, next year. The cows still had to be milked, the chickens fed, the grain threshed; just as if nothing had happened, and even though Henry would never do any of it with us again.

We found out later that his ship had been badly damaged somewhere off South America in the Battle of the River Plate. I'd never heard of the River Plate. Henry was killed trying to load a gun. I couldn't imagine Henry loading a gun.

Suddenly the war had a different face; it was real. People who were part of *our* lives could get killed in it. Henry had been the first, but who else would the war take? Stephen? Leonard? Dan?

Even our own family. If air raids came one of *us* might get killed, in spite of the Anderson shelter.

The pantomime rehearsals went on too. Dan was the Dame, and Rosa danced better all the time; her face lost its pinched look and sometimes she seemed almost happy. Bridget wasn't happy, though, I was sure of that.

Then school closed and it was Christmas.

'Is it all right for us to enjoy Christmas when Henry's dead?' I asked Mum.

We'd finished dinner and everyone was sitting round the fire and the Christmas tree, in the living room. Tom had a new model Spitfire. He ran round the room and between the chairs, falling over people's legs and making zooming noises interrupted with short staccato bursts of machine gun fire.

'That's *enough*,' Dad said. 'Sit down, Tom, for heaven's sake, and give us a bit of peace!'

I couldn't prevent myself enjoying Christmas, I thought, with Tom home again. And Mum had gone to so much trouble to make it as good as ever that it would have seemed ungrateful to do anything else. She'd hunted all over town to find enough raisins and sultanas for the cake and she'd been saving up sugar for weeks, whenever she could get it; people were saying there would be rationing before the end of January.

All the same. . . .

'Yes,' Mum said, as if she had no doubts. 'It is all right. Henry would want us to enjoy ourselves.'

Every Christmas afternoon as far back as I could remember Bridget and Dan and their parents had come over to visit us. I was a little anxious in case this year, with the war and whatever was wrong with Bridget, they might not come. But they did; exactly on time at four o'clock there they were on our doorstep, saying 'Happy Christmas', and stamping the snow off their shoes. They'd brought presents too, just as usual, a tin of toffees and some of Mrs Skerries' own shortbread, and tobacco for Dad. Our presents for them were wrapped up and waiting under the tree: the same tobacco they'd brought Dad for Mr Skerries, and a Madeira cake and a box of biscuits.

Then Mum made tea in the big brown earthenware teapot and cut the Christmas cake, and everybody laughed a lot and talked all at the same time. Dad threw extra logs on to the fire and they crackled and flamed and sent bursts of sparks flying up the chimney and everything felt warm and happy and secure. The war stayed outside and far away, and I could almost pretend it wasn't happening.

'Come and see my presents,' I invited Bridget.

We sat under the fairy lights on the Christmas tree, among bright, crumpled pieces of wrapping paper.

'A *camera*,' she said, impressed.

'Yes, isn't it super? From Mum and Dad. Would you like

67

to borrow it, sometimes? And Hazel gave me the five-year diary and the paints are from Tom.... Now tell me what you got.'

'The best thing of all was a make-up case. Powder in little pink tins, and lipstick and nail-polish, everything. . . .'

But somehow she didn't sound excited about it, as the old Bridget surely would have been, and when she added, 'You can use it when you want to, Peg,' there was an odd uncertainty in the glance she flicked towards me under her lashes, as if she wasn't sure I *would* want to. As if she was afraid I might not —

The doorbell rang, cutting in.

'Whoever can that be?' asked Mum. Dad went to answer it and we waited, rather quietly after all the chatter and noise; there were voices in the hall and then Dad came back, ushering the new neighbours in front of him.

Mr and Mrs Colfax, and Leonard, splendid in his RAF uniform.

I reached out a hand before I could stop myself and squeezed Bridget's.

Lucky Bridget, with Leonard home unexpectedly on Christmas leave; if only Stephen had got home too.

Her hand was cold and to my astonishment she didn't look pleased at all. Her face had gone dead white. 'Oh damn,' she said, very softly, so that under cover of all the greetings nobody heard but me. 'Damn, damn, *damn* —'

'I don't understand,' I whispered. 'I thought you liked Leonard a lot?'

'Liked *Leonard*?' She was staring at me, her eyes burning in her white face. 'You're crazy. I don't like Leonard at all. I *hate* him —'

She disengaged her fingers from mine and stood up.

'You can't hate somebody who's in the Services,' I protested. 'After all, he's fighting for his country!'

'Putting on a uniform doesn't change a person,' she snapped in a fierce whisper. 'He's just as horrible as ever. Worse, even —' Then she turned and walked away from me, shaking back her hair, and went across the room to Dan and her parents.

'Say Merry Christmas to Mrs Colfax, Bridget,' said her father.

'Merry Christmas,' said Bridget expressionlessly.

'I hope we're not intruding,' said Mrs Colfax. 'In Yorkshire we always went visiting on Christmas afternoon.'

'Of course not,' said Mum. 'We're delighted to see you.'

Then Mrs Colfax noticed Tom.

'Oh, Mrs Price! You're not going to tell me you've brought him home. . . . Just for Christmas, of course?'

'No,' said Mum. 'For good.'

Mrs Colfax's mouth became very small and disapproving in her large face. 'Oh, but I don't think you should have done that, Mrs Price! We'd all like our children to be at home, of course, but you really ought to consider Tom's safety. That's what matters most. I wouldn't even think of taking Joanie back —'

'I think what matters most is the family being together,' said Mum.

'I'd rather be at home,' put in Tom firmly.

'Tom will just take his chance with the rest of us,' Mum said, smiling at him. 'And now I must go and make some fresh tea.'

I felt proud of her, standing up to Mrs Colfax like that. And she was right, of course. She was always right.

Mrs Colfax sat down bulkily on the sofa, shaking her head, and helped herself to a piece of cake. 'Anyway,' she said as she munched, 'we've got our Leonard home for a few days. He's in the middle of his flying training, you know.'

'Yes,' said Mr Skerries, and cleared his throat. 'Well done.'

'Thanks,' said Leonard.

Dan had given Mr Colfax his seat and gone over to the window, and Hazel said, 'I'll see if Mum needs any help,' and slipped out to the kitchen.

Somehow the warm Christmas atmosphere had drained away, and conversation was awkward and stilted. I wished the Colfaxes hadn't come.

Then Hazel brought in the teapot and went round filling up cups, and Mum followed her with extra sandwiches, and everybody began to relax and enjoy themselves once again.

'Well well, a Spitfire!' Leonard said, laughing and ducking his head as Tom, tired of sitting still, zoomed in his direction. 'Just like mine!'

Tom stopped with his arm over his head in mid-flight. 'Can you fly a *Spitfire*?'

'I'm learning,' said Leonard.

'Boy!' said Tom.

Mum sighed. 'Stephen, Leonard, all these lads. One after the other. I suppose you'll be the next to join up, Dan.'

Dan finished his mouthful of cake and then said, quite easily and pleasantly even though his face was flushed, 'Well, as a matter of fact, no. I won't be going into the Services. I'm a conscientious objector.'

There was a sudden flat silence; it was so quiet you could hear a small blue flame hissing round the new log Dad had just put on the fire.

Then Leonard laughed.

'Always one of them, isn't there? And always so high-minded about it. As if any of us actually enjoyed the idea of killing—'

'Conshie — *what*?' I asked.

Everybody else seemed to know what it meant. The adults looked troubled, embarrassed, and Bridget's face was angry and defiant.

'Consci -en -tious ob -ject -or,' Leonard said carefully; the split syllables came out like a sneer.

'C.O.'s — people who object to fighting,' Dad explained hurriedly. 'Because of their conscience, Peg. They believe it's wrong.'

'There is another word for it, of course,' said Leonard. 'That begins with "CO" as well. . . .'

Dan didn't try to defend himself. He just stood there quietly in the window and I knew he'd listened to all this, every word of it, before.

Somebody had to speak up for him.

'If you mean *coward*,' I shouted furiously at Leonard, 'you'd better shut right up! That's about the stupidest thing I ever heard anyone say. A coward is one thing Dan most certainly is *not* —'

'Peg, really!' Mum interrupted me. 'You mustn't speak to Leonard like that. He's a guest in our house! And besides—'

'Dan's a guest too,' Hazel said. 'And he's got a perfect right to do what he thinks he ought to. I agree with Peg.'

So Hazel was on our side!

Thanks, I telegraphed silently across the room as our eyes met. Oh Hazel, thanks—

And unexpectedly the black cloud of jealousy and unhappiness that I'd been carrying around with me all these weeks began to lift, to lighten, to roll away. What mattered wasn't, after all, Hazel and Stephen; it was *Hazel and me!*

I'd got my sister back.

And Bridget, too. Because now I knew what had been the matter with Bridget: she'd been afraid we'd turn against Dan when we found out he was a C.O. Perhaps she'd even thought we might turn against her. But now she was smiling at me, a twisted, relieved smile with the old Bridget showing through as she blinked back tears, and she came and sat down beside me again.

The party didn't last long after that. Mum steered the conversation on to the shortage of torch batteries and elastic; then Mrs Colfax got up and said they'd better go. The Skerries followed.

'Peg, I've got something to say to you.'

I'd never heard that tone from Mum before, not to anyone, certainly not to me. Dad gave her one quick glance and then jerked his head at Tom, beckoning. 'Come on, son. Chickens to feed.'

I faced her across the litter of empty cups and cake crumbs that strewed the livingroom. The tree still glowed in its corner, the fire still crackled. A scarlet paper hat lay where it had fallen. Hazel picked it up, smoothing it with her fingers.

Mum said, 'Rudeness like that was absolutely unfor-givable, Peg.'

The controlled quietness of her voice only emphasized the fierce, leashed anger stamping in her eyes. It scared me. Surely I hadn't done anything *that* serious?

'I'm sorry if . . .' I began.

'How could you say such things to a neighbour's son? And at Christmas — when he's only home for a few days! When he's wearing the King's uniform —'

My own temper leaped. 'But Leonard practically called Dan a coward!'

'Yes, and with good reason!'

'That's unfair,' said Hazel.

Mum whipped round to face her instead. 'And that's another thing. I don't understand you either, Hazel! Siding with a miserable conshie when your own boyfriend is on active service — what on earth would Stephen say?'

'I don't know. Perhaps he'd say what I do, that Dan is doing what he thinks is right —'

'Or saving his skin,' Mum said scornfully.

'No!' I rushed in. 'Dan isn't like that! He has different ideas, that's all, and he stands up for them. Like being against birdnesting.'

'Different ideas — I should say so,' Mum retorted. 'Different from all the other boys who aren't afraid to go and fight for their country when it needs them!'

'Dan isn't *afraid*. I know he isn't. You're just being prejudiced —'

'*Peg!*' Mum's face was amazed and hurt, as if she couldn't believe I'd said a thing like that. I didn't care.

'Yes, you are!' I heard myself shouting. 'You're as bad as Mademoiselle! And you told me yourself it was wrong to be narrow-minded about Germans —'

'Conshies,' said Mum, 'are *entirely* different.'

'That's stupid!'

'Peg, you're being insolent. How dare you —'

'People aren't wrong, or wicked, just because they disagree with you! You said yourself there are two sides to every argument —'

'*Insolent*!' repeated Mum. She sounded breathless. 'It's that boy's influence! It must be!'

'That isn't fair—'

'You're not to have anything more to do with Dan, do you understand, Peg? You're not to see him or talk to him — ever again!'

'But I can't help seeing him!' I said, panicking. 'I have to see him. He's in the pantomime!'

'Oh.' For a moment she just stared at me, looking just as upset as I felt myself. 'All right, Peg, I suppose you can't help seeing him in the pantomime. But once that's over you're not to talk to him again, is that quite clear? I'm not prepared to have any daughter of mine mixed up with a conshie.'

It was a dreadful ending to Christmas Day. Even making up with Hazel, even having Tom home with us again, couldn't compensate for that terrible row with Mum.

I twisted and tossed all night long, trying to blot out her angry voice, echoing still inside my head, and my own furious answers. It was no use. They kept coming back even in my dreams, making me sweat and burn with shame and heartache.

'*Insolent.*'

How could I have been insolent to my Mum? I *loved* her. And how could the things you said come out so different from what you really meant?

I hadn't felt insolent, not even at the time. Only hurt and frightened because we were quarrelling. Surely she must have understood that?

In the morning, I told her I was sorry.

73

The River Tree is naked now.

I climb into the high fork among the stiff bare branches and look down past the tracery of brown twigs skinned with ice into the water swirling far below. Dead leaves and bits of debris, the shells of acorns, yellowing wisps of grass, sweep past in the current. A knife-edged wind buffets the deserted boughs.

Today the light is wrong; nothing is illuminated or transfigured today. I can't see the estuary, the sky is the colour of putty, and all the birds have flown away.

Growing up is lonely; one of the things you have to do by yourself.

Growing up hurts.

Only four months ago the war was just breaking out. Only four months ago, I knew where I belonged: inside my family. And everything I needed was there, inside my family, too.

Now everything is changing, because *I* am changing. There is a part of me, now, that belongs to other people.

Think about that, Peg Price, DJZJ Sixty-nine Four. Part of you belongs to Rosa. It was Mum herself who showed me that, Mum who said I must help Rosa find a place in the community; Mum who thought Rosa had a claim on me. . . .

The wind sharpens and a flurry of snow whitens the fields. The River Tree shakes its boughs silently, leaning with the wind.

Other people claim me too.

Bridget.

Dan. And Mum has said I must not have anything more to do with him. . . .

How can I know which way to go when I am torn between my family and my friends?

New Year, nineteen-forty; the coldest January anyone could remember.

Icicles hung in rigid silver fringes from the eaves, water pipes froze, the house smelt of paraffin heaters. Only the kitchen and the cowshed felt warm. Rationing began.

And on her eighteenth birthday Hazel joined the Wrens.

Dad said there was more than enough work for her on the farm and he didn't know how he'd manage. Mum said she was proud of Hazel and Dad musn't stand in her way. He could find someone else to do the farmwork.

As for me, I never seemed to have a spare minute. Pantomime rehearsals were held every day now. They grew more and more frantic and disorganized as the performance date drew nearer, and Mum, when she wasn't at the Red Cross, spent all her free time making my costume; almost, I sometimes thought, as if she was trying to make it up to me about Dan.

My costume was green, a gorgeous ghoulish Genie green with daubs of luminous paint, fitting tightly all over from the neck to the wrists and ankles. She had some difficulty over the fit; she couldn't track down a single zip fastener in any of the shops, and buttons didn't have the same effect. But when it was finished both of us were delighted with the result.

And then at last it was the dress rehearsal. Until now we'd rehearsed in late afternoon when school was over or on Saturday mornings. This time, Mr Gill wanted everything exactly as it would be on the night.

He fussed around in his shirtsleeves trying out new arrangements with the lighting while Mrs Pinckney did our make-up, rubbing our faces with sticks of greasepaint, drawing in lines, highlighting chins and cheekbones; everything became more and more chaotic as the evening wore on. Nothing seemed to go right. The dancers were out of step, Aladdin fluffed her lines, Buttons put a foot through the Dame's skirt (Bridget whispered that it was deliberate) and the spotlight fused.

I thought Mr Gill would blow a fuse himself, but he looked astonishingly cheerful. Mrs Pinckney said it was good luck for the dress rehearsal to be a disaster, and nobody was to worry.

At ten o'clock Rosa was collected by car; Mrs Brownrigg was nervous about her walking home in the dark. She offered Bridget and me a lift but neither of us accepted. It was far more fun to troop down the road with the rest of the cast, singing, excited, linked arm in arm.

I found myself squeezed in between Bridget and Dan. The night was freezing, with a million stars sparkling brilliantly all across the sky and only a thin new moon like a curl of lemon rind. An owl hooted as we passed under a tree, and when I glanced up every tiny twig was furred with frost; our feet crunched on the hard ground and long beams from half a dozen torches speared into the darkness ahead, crossing each other, bobbing up and down as we sang, 'Run, Rabbit, Run!'

Then Dan said, 'Wait a minute — what was that?' and in the silence that followed a deep voice growled out of the hedge, 'What do you think you're doing, showing all those lights?'

'Mr Warburton!' I said, guiltily.

'That's right,' Mr Warburton said. 'ARP. It won't do, you know, it won't do at all. One torch is quite enough. Pointed at the ground!'

'But there are fifteen of us,' Dan protested. 'And it's dark!'

'And what if Jerry spots you and drops a bomb?'

'That's silly,' said Annabelle. 'We haven't had a single raid in all these months and months!'

Mr Warburton said severely, 'The first could come tonight, young lady.'

'I bet it doesn't,' said Annabelle. 'It's the most boring war I ever heard of. That's why they call it the Phoney War, because nothing ever happens.'

Yes, it does, I thought, shivering suddenly. Henry. . . .

'As an Air Raid Warden it's my responsibility to see that people don't show lights,' said Mr Warburton. 'Raids or no raids. It's the law.'

'Of course,' said Dan. 'Sorry.'

Most of the torches had been switched off now, and the few still shining were pointed obediently downward, making small circular patches of light on the road.

'That's better,' said Mr Warburton. He climbed on to his bicycle and pedalled away and we went on, more quietly, to the crossroads. Then the crowd broke up and Bridget and Dan and I turned into the final mile, still arm in arm.

The road seemed longer at night, unfamiliar. Shadows blurred the bushes into bulky shapes and there were rustlings and squeakings you never heard by day. A bat staggered past us in a drunken zigzag fight; somewhere in the distance a dog was howling.

I was glad I had company.

Then we reached the Skerries' cottage. 'You go in, Bridget,' said Dan. 'I'll see Peg safely home.'

Sometimes I'd wondered how it would feel to be out alone with a boy. That was the point where all my dreams of Stephen always stopped, because I didn't know how to go on: what would I talk about? Well, here I was, alone with Dan. 'After the pantomime you're not to talk to Dan any more,' Mum had said, but this wasn't after. Not yet.

We talked about the pantomime, and Mr Gill; how his face had gone shiny with perspiration when the spotlight cracked up; how somehow Mrs Pinckney could always cope. Then I found myself explaining about Rosa, how she hadn't been fitting in, how the pantomime had helped.

'Good for you, Peg,' Dan said. Then he laughed. 'You used to be such a funny little girl, always disappearing or scrambling up trees, hiding away—'

'I still do,' I confessed, and told him about the River Tree, I wasn't sure why. 'I like to *think*,' I ended; it wasn't much of an explanation.

He said, 'I know what you mean. Getting ideas sorted out. . . .'

'Oh, you do understand! Hardly anyone does — they think I'm peculiar, wanting to be by myself. Mum gets worried about it. Or else they think I'm trying to get out of things, work and all that.'

Dan's arm tightened a little in mine. 'I've been doing some thinking myself, as a matter of fact.'

I said timidly, 'About being a C.O.?'

'Yes, about being a C.O.' I glanced at his face; it was serious, but not ashamed. Not ashamed at all. 'Taking life is something I will not do,' Dan said quietly. 'Any life.'

'But doesn't it scare you? Being *different* like that? Standing out against what other people expect you to do — having everyone against you?'

'Yes.' There was a pause and then he added, 'Remember when we played truth and honour, on your birthday?'

'I remember. You wouldn't tell. . . .'

'That was my scare, Peg. Having everyone against me.'

'Oh, Dan.' And his scare had come true. I could feel the strength running out of my fingertips as I tried to imagine what it must be like. Everyone against you. . . . 'But your parents,' I said, gropingly. 'Surely they. . . .'

'It's difficult for them. Embarrassing. When they see other people's sons in uniform— Well, look at Christmas afternoon.'

'And Bridget,' I said. I knew how Bridget had felt. Dan had stood out against all of them, alone.

I wanted to tell him how it only proved how brave he was, how much to be respected because he stood up for his principles, but somehow I couldn't. It would have seemed an impertinence.

And then Dan said, 'Sometimes I think about you, Peg. About how pretty you are —'

'*Pretty*? Me?'

He burst out laughing. 'Didn't you know?'

'But Hazel's the one who's pretty!'

'Well, of course she is, if you like chocolate-box

prettiness, all fluffy and romantic.'

'Doesn't everyone?' I asked.

We'd reached our back-door, and I hadn't even noticed. He opened it for me just the slenderest crack.

'Not everyone,' he said. 'Mind the blackout. Personally, I prefer a crop of freckles and a bit of character. . . . You, in fact! Goodnight, Peg!'

The house lights dimmed into darkness. Out in front the audience rustled and whispered; the orchestra began playing, the curtains swept back and the dancers, in their brilliantly coloured Persian costumes, sprang into the opening sequence. We were on.

I squinted through a crack in the side of my huge lamp. At the right moment I had to leap out of it in a cloud of green smoke from the thunder flashes that Mr Gill would let off in the wings, and meantime I had the best view of anyone in the hall. I could even pick out Mum in the audience, clapping and smiling.

The Art Department had made the scenery and it was fabulous. Painted flats showed the inside of the Sultan's palace, with marble statues and brocaded walls; a real staircase led up and down from a gilded cardboard balcony. The whole stage smelt excitingly of paint and dust and the powder Mrs Pinckney had shaken all over the floor to make it smooth for the dancers' feet.

And she'd been right about a disastrous dress rehearsal bringing good luck, I thought; it was going marvellously. I'd never seen the dancers as good, and even Rosa was responding to the audience as they clapped again and again. Dan clumped around as the Dame, whisking up his layers of frilled petticoats to show heavy football boots and legs as hairy as Mr Gill could have hoped, and the audience roared. The Princess looked so meltingly beautiful that you almost forgot she was Felicity.

Then Aladdin sat in a corner of the stage, alone and forlorn, cleaning the palace lamps. One of them was old and dirty, hardly worth cleaning. Aladdin began rubbing it and I crouched ready to leap, my heart banging. Any moment—

The thunder flash exploded, and I sprang.

But the green smoke didn't clear almost at once, as it should have done. Instead it thickened, filling the stage with a bitter, choking reek, and there were gasps from the audience as Mr Gill staggered out from behind the curtain with his hands to his face.

I was nearest, so I reached him first. Aladdin turned into Annabelle again and ran towards us screaming, and then Mrs Pinckney and Dan rushed out to help as we steered Mr Gill behind the scenes.

His face was black and so was his shirt, his sports jacket torn and smeared. He flapped his hands at us. 'Don't *fuss*. I'm all right. Just shaken up, nothing more —'

'Your eyebrows are singed right off,' said Mrs Pinckney, as we helped him into a chair. 'Can you see properly?'

'Of course I can see. I keep telling you I'm all right—'

'Good,' said Mrs Pinckney. 'Felicity, get some lint and a bowl of water. Then we'll see what the damage is. And Dan, go out on the stage and tell the audience we won't be long and we're sorry for the delay. Then ring down the curtain and put up the house lights.'

'It's these damned wartime substitutes,' Mr Gill grumbled irritably. 'Ersatz this, ersatz that — you never know what you're getting these days. You'd think at least in wartime they could manage proper explosives.'

'They did,' said Annabelle, giggling nervously. 'It's the fake bit that didn't work—'

'If you will like,' another voice said shyly, 'it is not quite necessary to draw down the curtain. To occupy the audience if you like it I will entertain—'

'What?' said Mrs Pinckney.

'Dance.' Rosa's face, strangely audacious, keyed-up, looked out at us from her bright orange costume. 'I will dance, and the audience will be engaged till the performance comes back.'

'That's a good idea,' said Dan.

Mrs Pinckney nodded. 'Yes, all right. Get the orchestra

going again, too.' She turned as Felicity came back carrying a bowl and cotton wool, and took it from her. 'Now, George, just sit quietly and don't argue. And Peg, hold that for me and don't let it spill—'

She mopped deftly at Mr Gill's face, using fresh wads of cotton wool for each wipe; somewhere in the background I was aware of the orchestra playing again, and of a light clicking sound from the stage. Mr Gill wasn't as all right as he'd pretended. His face had gone grey, as if he might faint.

'My Mum is out there in the audience,' I said. 'She's in the Red Cross. Shall I get her?'

'Well. . . .' Mrs Pinckney considered it for a moment. 'We don't want to alarm people. But if you know where she's sitting, then perhaps. . . .'

I knew exactly. 'Almost beside the centre aisle, in the fourth row.'

Nobody was looking at me as I slipped down the side steps from the stage, past the piano and the violins and between the rows of chairs. Even Mum seemed to have her attention on something else.

'What? Oh, Peg — it's you, dear!'

'Could you come backstage with me? Just for a moment?'

'Yes, of course.'

She got up and edged past the two seats between her and the aisle and somebody said, 'Sit down!' A woman in a red hat grumbled, 'Why some people have to move about in the middle. . . .' I lost the rest, because I was taking Mum back the way I'd come.

And then I saw what was holding the attention of the audience and stopped, myself. I couldn't move.

Rosa was dancing.

Not dancing, exactly, more like a mixture, a blend, of tap-dancing and acrobatics. I'd never seen anything like it in all my life.

She was using every prop in the pantomime as if it had been provided just for her, vaulting from the staircase, lifting the tambourines and pirouetting with them, cartwheeling across the stage; turning the Genie's magic lamp onto its side, rolling it in a wide arc, meeting it, moving it under her tapping feet, as they took up and elaborated and enhanced the rhythm of the orchestra; and you knew, you could feel, that she hadn't thought out or rehearsed any of it beforehand, that every step had sprung that moment, newly invented, out of her spirit and her imagination.

Then the music came to an end and the whole audience rose to its feet, stamping and cheering and shouting for more.

I couldn't stay watching any longer, of course. I hurried Mum behind the scenes, the orchestra started up again and we could hear the tap of Rosa's dancing feet. 'No hurry,' I told Mrs Pinckney as Mum went to work on Mr Gill. 'Rosa will keep them happy all night.'

In fact she didn't need to. Mum had learned her stuff at those Red Cross classes. Mr Gill was soon looking better, and Mrs Pinckney decided the show could go on — though without the wartime thunderflashes. We'd had enough of them.

We took curtain call after curtain call. They clapped for the Dame, for the Genie, for the Princess, for Aladdin; they clapped the whole cast together as if they'd forgotten how to stop. They were a tremendous audience.

And then, when it really seemed over at last, somebody shouted, 'The dancer! We want the dancer!' and Mrs Pinckney pushed Rosa out in front, alone, and the audience went mad all over again.

After a little while, radiant and triumphant, she slipped back to join the rest of us and slid her hand into mine.

'Oh Rosa,' I whispered, 'you were wonderful! Why didn't you tell us you could dance like that?'

'But I could not,' she whispered back. 'Never, since. . . . It is you, Peg, is to thank.'

I wanted to tell her that was nonsense, but Miss Miller was coming on to make her speech.

We waited expectantly, and Miss Miller cleared her throat before she began.

'I know that every single one of you here must have been as moved as I was by this little girl's performance tonight. And I hope that Rosa will forgive me if I depart from what I had intended to say and tell you instead something of her story. . . .'

I could feel Rosa's fingers tightening among my own as her whole body tensed. But when I glanced at her face it wasn't scared or lonely any more, and her head was up, high and proud.

'Rosa came to us a few months ago, from Germany. She is a refugee.' Miss Miller spoke slowly and very quietly. You could feel the audience listening. 'Rosa is Jewish. Rosa is the only member of her family to have escaped Hitler and his concentration camps. She does not know what has happened to her mother or her father or her sister or her two brothers—'

I had never known a silence like the silence in the hall now. Miss Miller waited for a moment and let her words have their full effect. Then, in the same quiet voice, she went on.

'And yet Rosa danced for us here tonight. Danced in a way that none of us, I think, has ever experienced before. That is courage. And so I have taken leave to tell you Rosa's story, without asking her permission first, because I believe that tonight she has given us something of tremendous value. Because I believe we can each one of us take something of Rosa's courage for ourselves, and carry it with us through all the darkness and the dangers of war that may lie ahead. . . .'

13

'*No*, Richard!'

Mum's voice exploded out of her in furious indignation. Her face was dark red. 'I won't have it!' she went on. 'Not at any price! I simply will not accept it and that's that!'

I felt like crying, and Tom's spoon was clattering against his cornflake bowl as he stared at her in astonishment across the breakfast table.

'I don't care what you say, Richard, it's too much to ask of us. Much too much! Nobody could expect it, it isn't reasonable —'

'They do expect it,' Dad said, and added pacifically, 'Take it easy now, Dorothy!' He was still holding the letter in his hand, out of her reach, as if he was afraid she might snatch it and tear it up; he looked all hot and bothered.

'*Easy!*' Mum retorted. 'I tell you, I won't put up with it. I don't see why you're even considering it. The idea of taking on a conscientious objector to work on the farm when your own daughter is in the Wrens, risking her life —'

'Look,' said Dad. 'I need a cowman, right? And the authorities are sending me Dan. And Hazel isn't risking her life, that's an exaggeration. She's only stationed at Chatham, not twenty miles from home.'

'And what if the Germans bomb the dockyard? Don't you realise they might do that? They probably will, any day now —'

'Yes, well. . . .'

'I think it's great they're sending us Dan,' said Tom. 'After all, he is a friend!'

'No, he isn't,' said Mum. 'Not any more. Skulking behind a tractor—'

'That isn't fair!' I interrupted, trying to control the shake in my voice. It was April now and I'd hardly seen Dan since the pantomime, but that conversation as we walked home together from the dress rehearsal had stayed in my mind.

'Dan's not skulking,' I defended him. 'He's only trying to do what he thinks is right. And that must be desperately difficult when he knows that everybody else disagrees with him—'

'Well, I'm glad at least to hear you don't agree with him, Peg,' Mum said. Her voice was sharp. 'In the last war they sent white feathers to men who didn't join up. White feathers, meaning cowardice.'

'You *wouldn't*,' I said in horror. 'Oh Mum, you wouldn't do a thing like that. *Please.* . . .'

'No, I wouldn't. I didn't approve of that either. But I won't have a conshie working on our farm. You'll just have to look for somebody else, Richard.'

'I can't,' said Dad. 'I haven't any choice. Dan has been officially allocated to do essential farmwork by the Ministry of Employment and they're sending him to us. Now do you understand?'

'But I *won't*—'

'There's no point in saying that again, Dorothy. You'll have to do what you're told just like the rest of us. There's a war on.'

Everybody was using that phrase nowadays: There's a war on. Especially when things happened that they didn't like.

Mum gave up at last, defeated. 'Oh, all right then. If Dan has to come here, then I suppose he must.' She pressed her lips together in a hard, tight line. 'But don't expect me to like it, Richard. And you'll have to give him your instructions yourself, because I have no intention of speaking to him, not ever again.'

I grated back my chair from the table and stood up. Dad said, 'You haven't finished your breakfast, Peg!'

'I don't care. I don't want it.'

I couldn't eat any toast, not even with my butter ration on it. I felt scared and sick, and all I wanted was to get away.

I plunged out of the kitchen and across the yard, and then I slammed the barn door shut behind me and threw myself down in the hay. There was only a little hay left, in a corner;

spring was here and Easter holidays and daffodils and new lambs and baby chickens and little wobbly calves with soft brown eyes like the eyes of pansies — the time of year I liked best. But there was a war on. Henry had died in it, and Hazel had gone away and so had Stephen and Leonard, and Mum had changed into someone else, someone I hardly recognized, because of Dan; and everything — *everything* — was horrible.

I cried and cried and cried.

After a long time the barn door creaked gently open and then shut again, and somebody crept in, somebody snuggled beside me and put two arms round my neck and hugged me hard.

'Oh, *Tom*,' I said.

He let me go and just sat there, with me, in the dimness of the barn. The hay smelt sweet and dusty, and the specks of dust dived and flickered in the thin thread of sun that came through a crack in the door; the clank of buckets in the dairy sounded far away.

After a while Tom went over to the ladder in the corner and climbed up it to the loft, and when he came down he was carrying something very carefully in his arms.

'Three, Peg — look. Misty had them last night while you and Mum were milking.'

'Already? I thought she'd be another week, at least.'

'Lucky I found her. She was in the wheelbarrow behind the old cart. Look quickly, Peg, in case somebody comes.'

The kittens squirmed in my hands, scraps of mewing black fur, already arching their tiny tails. 'Oh, aren't they darling. We'll have to look for homes for them, Tom. Perhaps Rosa would be allowed to have one.'

'As long as they're not drowned. . . . Are you better now?'

'Yes. I'm fine.'

He looked relieved. 'Oh, good. Peg . . . there's something I don't understand. Doesn't Mum like Dan any more?'

'It's not that she doesn't like him, exactly,' I said slowly. 'It's just this war. It seems to have changed everything.'

'But you do like Dan, Peg, don't you?'

'Yes, of course. Of course I do—'

'Good,' said Tom. 'Because I like him, too.'

Dan came to work for us the next day, and Mum kept her word.

Dan and I did the milking, and even Mum saw it wasn't reasonable to expect me not to talk to him. She said it was all right, she supposed, but only when we were working together.

Mum looked after the dairy and the chickens and the calves, and Dad and Dan between them did the fieldwork.

Dan went home for his dinner.

When Mum made a cup of tea, at mid-morning or in the afternoon, Dan got his like everyone else, and a sandwich or a piece of cake like everyone else too.

But she didn't speak to him, she didn't ever smile at him or do anything that could possibly be seen as making him welcome, not in any way at all.

Not once.

A week after Dan arrived the war stopped being phoney and turned real. We heard on the radio that Hitler's armies had invaded Denmark and Norway, both on the same day, and British forces were rushing to their aid.

I could feel a new, prickling excitement in the atmosphere. At last, after months of delay, the war was on the move. This time we'd show Hitler, Dad said, with satisfaction, this time he'd bitten off more than he could chew.

But Dad was mistaken. Hitler, it turned out, had no difficulty chewing Denmark, and not much more chewing Norway; it was the Germans who 'showed' us.

Tom and I could hardly take it in, until the day Annabelle's family got a message to come and visit her brother. He was in a military hospital near London with his right arm smashed to bits.

'Denmark and then Norway lost in three weeks,' Dad growled furiously as he stamped up and down the kitchen in his boots. He'd come straight in from planting hops to hear the six o'clock evening news; the marvellous spring weather was still holding, and he and Dan were making the most of it, using every daylight hour. 'We licked old Jerry all right in the last lot, what's gone wrong now? It's this blasted government. Crowd of useless pussyfooting old women — What's happened to *Great* Britain?'

Tom and I had been wondering that too, and the thing that mattered more than anything else, to us, was what might happen now to Tom.

'Promise you won't send me away again,' he pleaded, clutching Mum's arm. 'Please, please. I want to stay at home with all of you, whatever happens in the war—'

'I promise,' said Mum. 'I couldn't bear you to go away any more, Tom.'

'Even if there's an invasion?'

'Even then. I promise.'

'Then everything is all right,' said Tom.

'Don't suppose that load of old idiots could even organize resistance against an invasion,' Dad said disgustedly, and stamped out of the house to the hopfield.

But the entire atmosphere changed almost overnight, when early in May Hitler invaded Holland and Belgium and we got a new Prime Minister: Winston Churchill.

I wouldn't have believed it possible for one person to have so much effect.

Inspiration, Mum called it; it was as if a huge unexpected wave of energy had been unleashed and was pounding all through the nation. You could see the difference in people's faces, in the way they acted; in Dad, for instance. He wasn't angry now, and he never seemed to get tired however hard or however long he worked. He tramped around the place whistling, and he looked almost young.

One sunny evening Mr Churchill spoke to us on the radio. Mum and Dad sat beside the set, heads bent intently towards it as they listened; Tom stayed near them and I settled myself on the back step with the kitchen door open so I could hear. Dan came and stood beside me.

The deep powerful voice, the marvellous sonorous phrases rolled on. He is speaking to me, I thought. Not merely to a mass of invisible unidentified people but to each separate one of us, to *me*. His words flamed in my heart and set me alight; I longed with everything in me to rush out and meet the challenge that he set us, to struggle and battle and win through.

'One bond unites us all,' the voice was saying. 'To wage war until victory is won, and never surrender ourselves to servitude. . . .' I glanced up at Dan, all of a sudden burningly aware of his presence at my side. I'd never seen his face so serious. His jaws were clamped rigid and deep lines scored themselves above his brows. I wanted to reach out my hand to his and hold it, to grip it hard, but I didn't dare.

'As conquer we must,' the voice finished at last. 'As conquer we shall.'

There was complete, utter silence.

Then the announcer said, 'That was the Prime Minister, the Right Honourable Winston Churchill,' and somebody clicked off the radio.

Dan turned abruptly without a word and walked away towards his bicycle, propped against the cowshed wall.

I could hear Mum calling from the kitchen, 'Time you came in, Peg, it's getting cold,' but I didn't answer. Something else mattered more.

'Wait for me, Dan. Please wait. Don't go off just like that! Please —'

He paused for a moment with one leg swung over the bar of his bicycle. 'Go home, Peg. Your mother's calling you.'

'I don't care.'

'Well, I do.' His voice sounded harsh; angry and bitter. 'She doesn't like you talking to me when you don't have to, and I don't blame her. She's entitled to feel like that. After all I'm a conshie!'

I said stumblingly, 'Well, but you have to do what you think is right . . .'

He went a dark, fierce red. 'Yes, I damned well do have to. But farmwork, for God's sake. Bloody farmwork, and *here*

89

of all places in the world—'

I took a step backwards; it felt as if he'd slapped me in the face.

'Dan, don't you like working for us?'

He was glaring at me as if I didn't understand a thing.

'I'll show them,' he said savagely. 'You wait. One day I'll show them. The whole bloody lot—'

'Including me?' I retorted, my anger boiling up. If he couldn't see I was on his side I wasn't the girl to tell him, not in a hundred years. Not in a hundred thousand —

'Especially you!' shouted Dan, and left me standing there in the farmyard, staring after him, as he pedalled furiously away.

14

Thick black arrows struck south and west from Germany across the map of Europe.

We stared down at it on the front page of the *Daily Express*, crowding round Mrs Pinckney's desk as she spread it out for us to see. It was Wednesday, when we began with double English, but Current Events had taken the place of English now.

The arrows were German armies, German tanks.

There was a terrible excitement in watching. Each day the arrows dug deeper, nearer; each day the patch of France that contained the B.E.F. shrank smaller and smaller, until now it was only a narrow strip beside the coast.

Felicity said with her usual cocksureness, 'Well, we're bound to push the Germans back soon. I mean, we're *bound* to. There isn't any chance of us *losing* the war—'

'Isn't there?' asked Mrs Pinckney.

She was pale, and dark smudges underlined her eyes. Perhaps that dull intermittent rumble, like thunder rolling on the horizon, had kept her awake last night.

'Do you know anyone in the B.E.F., Mrs Pinckney?' I asked.

'Yes, I do, Peg.' She smiled, a smile like a shadow. 'My husband.'

Mrs Pinckney's husband, Nan's brother, Alice's Dad. And Stephen too, perhaps. . . .

Stephen, Stephen. He was Hazel's boyfriend, not mine, but it wouldn't hurt, I thought, if I said his name over and over in my heart, quietly, like a prayer. Stephen. And Leonard, in the RAF; he might be there too. And all the others; they weren't just soldiers or sailors or airmen, they were brothers and husbands and sons as well.

Mrs Pinckney nodded to me understandingly, as if the same thoughts were going through her head. 'The beloved army,' she said softly, as if she were saying it to herself.

Felicity didn't have anyone she loved, anyone near to her, in the B.E.F. She said indignantly, 'Of *course* we can't lose the war, and it's unpatriotic even to consider it. We're in the right so we can't lose. Everybody knows that!'

'"Victory in Our Just Cause",' quoted Bridget. 'That's what Miss Miller says every single day at morning prayers.'

There was an odd expression on Rosa's face. 'So you believe if you are in the right and Miss Miller is praying, there can be nothing go wrong for you?'

'Well, not exactly,' said Felicity. 'I suppose things are going wrong now, a bit. But in the end — it's bound to be all right in the end, isn't it? I mean, you've only got to imagine what would happen if Hitler won. God simply couldn't allow it—'

Rosa didn't answer. I wouldn't let myself think about the things God had allowed to happen to Rosa, or to her family.

Mrs Pinckney said very slowly, 'Have any of you ever considered that it might be God's will for us to lose the war?'

I stared at her in amazement.

'That's stupid,' said Felicity angrily.

'Is it?' asked Mrs Pinckney, and then added, 'I don't know. I simply do not know. . . .'

She really means that, I thought. *She doesn't know.* She doesn't know any more than I do, or Felicity. It occurred to me that this wasn't like a lesson, something between a teacher and a group of pupils, at all; it was more like a conversation between people who were perplexed and troubled, and trying to understand.

'But that turns everything upside down,' Felicity was saying. 'If evil can defeat good then nothing makes sense any more. I don't believe God would do a thing like that—'

'Perhaps,' said Mrs Pinckney, 'God's way of looking at the world is different from ours.'

The rumble in the distance laboured on through the morning and the afternoon, now building up, now fading to a sullen mutter, a fluctuating murderous accompaniment to the windless day.

School went on too. Not because it seemed to matter but merely because for everyone involved in it each succeeding lesson was simply the next thing that was there to be done. Nothing mattered any more except the army across the sea, the B.E.F.; except today and tomorrow: now, the immediate moment that had suddenly inflated into a looming inescapable eternity that engulfed us all and made anything outside itself empty of meaning or reality.

The same atmosphere of muted restlessness, of fear and anxiety, horrifying and yet shot through with the glitter of excitement, filled the town as we came out of school.

Small groups of people were knotted together in doorways or on street corners, and in the distance, carried across the water on the stifling windless air, the rumble grumbled on.

'It's strange,' I said to Bridget, really thinking out loud, 'I'm scared, but I wouldn't have missed it. I'm scared for all the soldiers and the sailors and the airmen who are out there fighting, I'm scared for us and all the other people who may get bombed and invaded and even killed — but even so, I wouldn't have missed it, I'm glad we're living now. *Now*, in May nineteen forty.'

Bridget caught my arm. 'Look, Peg, look. Down the road.'

They came in a column, marching from the direction of Dover; and yet it wasn't really like marching, not like a parade. All along the street people began to cheer them, crying, waving, running out into the broken lines to give them presents of biscuits, chocolate, anything that came to hand. The soldiers accepted the presents with weary thanks and came on, tramping, tramping up the street.

They were grimy, unshaven, half-clad. Some had no tunics, some were bare-headed, some were bootless, limping past in khaki socks or on feet wrapped in blood-stained rags. Some wore blackened bandages, eye-patches, slings; every one of them looked gaunt and exhausted and bruised and hammered to the bone. Some waved and one, a boy in a torn khaki sweater with leather patches at the elbows, sent me a dredged-up cheeky grin as he went past and shouted, 'Hi!' Most were quiet, moving mechanically, as if they were too tired to respond.

A middle-aged woman, standing beside me with tears running down her cheeks, called out to them, 'Tell us what's happening to our army. Tell us what it's like over there,' and a young redhaired soldier whose face had grown old told her.

'It's like hell, ma'am, that's what it's like. Hell beside the seaside. Just like hell itself.'

15

The River Tree wears chestnut flowers like white wax candles burning among its leaves. From the high fork in its branches, on this strange spring afternoon of fear and doubt and glittering sun, I can see far down the river. The light isn't right, the light is smudged with smoke; but still I can see as far as the bustling estuary, as far as the English Channel beyond.

And beyond that again, out of my sight, stretch the sandy beaches of France where at this very moment the war is raging at its fiercest and men are dying in sunshine and smoke and flame.

A tug goes hurrying past me towards the estuary, froth breaking white on either side, its wake spreading behind it in a rippling triangle; and smoke drifts black above the wake.

'Victory is certain,' Miss Miller says.

Always, ever since the war began, she's been sure of that. Absolutely sure. Our cause is just, so we will win: it's logical, like geometry.

But today, in school, *Mrs Pinckney wasn't sure*.

That means Miss Miller can be wrong.

Then anyone can be wrong, anyone at all.

Even my Mum.

A motor boat pulses past under the chestnut tree. On her deck is a man coiling rope; another man stacks tins into a locker. Both look wholly occupied, intent on what they are doing.

Perhaps nobody knows anything for absolutely certain. Perhaps in his deepest heart even Churchill doesn't *know* how this war will end.

Churchill, Miss Miller, Mrs Pinckney, Mum.

Unexpectedly I feel sorry for them. Under their outer confidence and authority, I begin to see, they too are anxious and confused. Why have I never realised that before?

Nobody 'knows'.

We are all groping our way through, then, trying to do what seems best, what's right. And what's right — that's something people can disagree about: like Mum and Dan.

And the world is more difficult, more dangerous, than I have ever understood.

A cabin cruiser slips past me down the river and the white candles rock in a gust of wind; I shiver, high above the water among the shifting patterns of sun and restless leaves.

More dangerous . . .

Truth and honour, what scares you most of all?

How would they have answered that question, all these adults I've always thought so infallible, so reliable, so sure? What answers could they have given if they'd joined in that game on my birthday?

The war; the war, that scares them all. They don't know what it will bring to them, they don't know how it will end.

The war scares me, too.

But there's nothing I can do about the war. The war is beyond my scope.

Except for one small thing. . . .

And what can I do about that? How can I tell, how can I decide, who's right — Mum, or Dan?

I can't decide. I don't know how to.

I am cold and lonely and afraid, and all around me the leaves of the River Tree are shaking and rustling in the wind.

Listen, listen, says the River Tree.

The branches sway and the candles tremble. Listen, says the whisper of the leaves, and slowly the whisper grows, filling the air; it swells and deepens and throbs until it becomes a clamour, until I can feel it rushing and roaring and vibrating all about me on every side.

Listen, listen, listen!

Listen to yourself, Peg Price, DJZJ Sixty-nine four: *Listen to yourself*!

Only you can decide what you must do.

That is what growing up means.

You make up your mind.

16

Mum was flaming mad, and I didn't blame her. I'd missed the evening milking altogether and everyone had finished supper; their places at the table had been cleared and the dishes washed and dried. In her place I'd have been mad myself.

She raged at me while I swallowed my sausages and mash.

'Whatever is the matter with you these days, Peg? I don't understand you. I simply do not understand you at all!'

The sausages were burnt with being heated up again and the potato was black on the outside and cold in the middle. Somehow I pushed it down.

'You used to be such a solid, dependable little girl — somebody I could rely on. Now all of a sudden — I tell you, I don't know what's come over you!'

'I'm sorry, Mum.'

'Don't talk with your mouth full! What have you been *doing*, all this time?'

'I wasn't doing anything.'

'You must have been doing something! You weren't out with that boy — no, of course you weren't! You couldn't have been.'

'I wasn't with anyone. I was just thinking.'

'How can anyone spend three hours *just thinking*?'

'I'm *sorry*!'

'You're always disappearing these days. Always! Especially when I need you to help. You've even got Tom doing it now!'

'Tom?' I asked in surprise.

'Yes, Tom! Just like you. He's disappeared as well — went out the minute he'd finished his supper with never so much as an if-you-please! I don't understand either of you any more!'

'I am sorry, Mum. Really I am—'

But she wasn't ready yet to accept an apology. 'Sorry isn't enough. You can just go up to your bedroom and stay there for the rest of the evening, Peg. Perhaps that'll teach you to have a bit more consideration for other people!'

So I sat alone at my bedroom window, with a French translation lying neglected in front of me on the table. Outside, the evening sun was dropping gradually down the sky, shading it from the palest blush overhead to a deep crimson on the horizon's curve, and in the far distance the menacing rumble came and went as it had all day. Somewhere close by me a thrush was singing.

I *was* sorry, though not for staying out late. I was sorry for Mum, who didn't understand me. She didn't understand Dan, either.

Ever since I could remember Dan had been a person who stood up for what he believed to be right. Even when no-one else agreed with him.

That starling's egg, for instance, long ago — Dan had made a stand over that. Just as, now, he was making a stand over being a conscientious objector, because he believed it was wrong to take life, ever.

It needed courage to stand up for your beliefs. A difficult kind of courage.

If only I could make Mum see.

It was because of Hazel, I thought, that she minded so much about Dan being a C.O. Perhaps it *was* difficult to be fair to a conshie when your own son or daughter was in the Services. Stephen's and Leonard's parents all felt the same as Mum.

Perhaps *they* needed understanding too. . . .

And just as that thought struck me I heard light footsteps come running up the stairs, and Tom opened the door into my room.

'Shhh!' he hissed at me warningly, and closed the door very quietly behind him. 'I don't want Mum and Dad to hear.' Then he tiptoed across the floor, sat down on Hazel's bed and leaned towards me.

'Peg — can you keep a secret?'

'Of all the silly questions I ever heard.'

'Well then, listen.' His eyes were almost crackling with excitement but somehow he looked wary, cautious, at the same time; I'd never seen him look like that before. 'It really is a secret, Peg. The biggest secret we've ever had.'

'Go on, then,' I said impatiently.

'It was the kittens, you see. Dad said at supper he was going to turn out the hayloft tomorrow morning, so I had to do something about the kittens right away. Well, you weren't there, Peg, and if Dad found them he might . . . you know. *Drown* them — so it was desperate.'

'Yes. Of course.'

Of course the kittens were important, but I couldn't help feeling a little let down. 'The biggest secret ever,' Tom had said — somehow, I'd expected more.

'Well,' said Tom again. 'I managed to get out of the house without anyone noticing, and I put the kittens into a box and made holes in the top for air—'

'Before you put the kittens in, I hope.'

'Don't be stupid, Peg. Then luckily I saw Dan. He'd been working late because one of the cows calved just before supper and he was clearing up. And he gave me a lift on his crossbar, with the kittens. It was super fun.'

'Did you manage to find homes for all of them?'

'Yes. Rosa took one like you suggested, and Dan dropped another off at his house and then we went on to Mr Warburton's. That was Dan's idea. And *that* was when—'

'Did Mr Warburton take a kitten?' I asked. 'Good for him!'

'What?' Tom seemed surprised at my question, as though his mind had already run on to something else. 'Well yes, he did, though at first I thought he might not because he was so busy. He said just to put it in his kitchen and he'd see to it later on. So I left it there in the box — I expect it'll be all right.'

There was something odd about this. 'Why was he so busy?' I wanted to know.

'Because he's been taking things down to all those boats

in the estuary,' Tom said. 'Things from the ARP stores. Bandages and bully beef and biscuits and all that.'

'But I thought those stores were for an emergency. For if the Germans start an invasion and we have to organise resistance?'

'Yes, that's what Dan said too, when Mr Warburton was explaining. But Mr Warburton says this *is* an emergency. He says everything has to go, because it's needed now.'

I couldn't make head or tail of it. 'Everything has to go *where*?'

'To France,' said Tom. 'That's where the boats are going. Every boat that can be found, Mr Warburton said. He said it was an appeal from the Chief of Naval Staff —'

'But why? I don't understand —'

'To bring back the B.E.F., of course.'

'Oh.' I felt suddenly rather dizzy. 'Is the war over, then? Have we *lost*?'

'I don't know,' Tom said impatiently. 'Anyway that isn't the secret. Swear you won't tell, Peg, or you'll spoil everything —'

'Yes, of course. I swear.'

'Dan is going too,' said Tom. 'In Stephen's boat.'

I stood staring at him while the words turned into meaning.

'With Dr Rutland?' I managed to whisper at last. I felt almost suffocated by happiness and terror, all jumbled up together so that I didn't know which was on top.

Dan was going to the war. Dan was as ready as anybody else to do his part: it was just that his part was different. 'Taking life is something I will not do,' he'd said. 'Any life.' And now he was going to war, not to take lives but to save them. To help bring home the B.E.F.

And soon all of them, Mum and Leonard and Stephen's parents and Leonard's parents and everyone else, would know that Dan wasn't afraid.

Tom was still explaining. 'Well, not exactly *with* Dr Rutland. That's why it has to be a secret, you see. Dr Rutland happens to be away, in London.'

'Then I don't quite . . .'

'Dan is sort of borrowing the boat.'

'Sort of . . . You mean, Stephen's mother doesn't know either?'

'She might have said no. Dan couldn't afford to ask her, not when every single boat is needed. And Mr Warburton thought it was an absolutely great idea. Peg, you swore you wouldn't tell!'

'Of course I won't tell!' I said indignantly.

But there was something I had to tell Dan — now, tonight, before he went. Because there might not be another chance; like Henry, Dan might not come back.

'Tom, how long?'

Tom narrowed his eyes consideringly. 'Well, Mr Warburton did say they're under starters' orders already. But the boat hasn't been out since last summer, and Dan would have to load up with food and petrol and bandages and all that. . . .'

Bandages. War. Torn flesh, shattered bone—

My throat ached, and fear stamped up and down inside my stomach.

'Come on,' I said, pulling a heavy sweater out of the cupboard, and over my head. 'We'll have to hurry.'

We slipped downstairs and past the closed door of the livingroom. I could hear Mum and Dad talking behind it, but this wasn't the time for explaining or asking permission. I'd put that right with Mum tomorrow, and make her understand. Surely she would, when it was so urgent: the most urgent, the most desperately important thing in all my life.

In the pantry I searched hastily for something to give to Dan. Apples, a tin of sardines, some cheese; they'd have to do. I stuffed them into a string bag and we let ourselves out into the cool, quiet night.

Shep was curled up on the other side of the farmyard. He got up and stretched and padded over to us, wagging his tail and cocking his ears expectantly.

'Come on, then!' I said. It was simpler than telling him to stay, and I didn't want him to start barking. The less attention we attracted, the better.

'Tell you what,' I said. 'The trench! Just in case Mum or Dad happen to look out of the window and see us running down the garden.'

It was the first time that trench had come in useful since we made it.

In five minutes we had crossed the paddock on to Dr Rutland's land and reached the river bank. The sky was darkening now and here and there a star showed. As we went past the River Tree its leaves were rustling, as they had rustled all round me this afternoon.

'Thanks,' I whispered back to it under my breath.

'One thing I don't quite understand,' said Tom. 'I used to think it was Stephen you had a thing about.'

'Oh — Stephen.'

How strange. I tried to recapture the way I'd felt about Stephen, and I couldn't. The feeling had gone.

'Stephen's super,' I said slowly. 'But it's Stephen and Hazel, you know, Tom. Not Stephen and me.'

'That's good,' said Tom with satisfaction.

There were many boats on the river now, slipping past us in the deepening dusk as the tug and the motorboat and the cabin cruiser had passed me hours ago. We hurried on, skirting the end of Stephen's garden, keeping to the shadows. The blackout curtains were tightly drawn in the big white house.

Except for that intermittent rumbling in the distance the evening was quiet, almost peaceful.

Then we were on the path to the jetty and there in front of us, creaking as she swung against her mooring, was *Excalibur*. And Dan, wearing oilskins and bending over something in her stern.

At first he didn't even notice us.

His long brown fingers were roping a tarpaulin, stashing it in the stern locker. Like those other men earlier he was working with total absorption, as if nothing mattered except what he had to do now.

Then Shep ran along the jetty and jumped into the boat and licked Dan's hand, and he glanced up and saw Tom and me coming towards him.

'Hi,' said Tom.

Dan was furious. 'What in the *hell* — Tom, I told you not to tell anybody! Not *anybody*!'

'Peg isn't "anybody",' Tom said in surprise. 'Anyway, I made her swear she wouldn't let on. And she hasn't seen a single soul except Shep since I told her.'

'Even so!'

Dan was glaring at me now; I'd stopped half a dozen yards away. For some reason I felt suddenly shy.

'We thought you might need some help,' I said. 'And we brought you a few things. Here—'

The taut lines of his face relaxed a little. 'Well — thanks. You may as well come alongside. Hurry up . . . Just keep your voices down, both of you, in case some idiot hears and makes difficulties.'

He still wasn't pleased we'd come, I thought. I really hadn't reckoned on that.

I handed him down the string bag and he peered into it before stuffing it in the locker beside the tarpaulin. 'Apples, h'm. Decent of you . . . Now, do you think you can roll that petrol drum over here between you? As long as you came to help.'

We rolled the drum over the side of the jetty and Dan eased it down into the boat and then wiped his hands on his oilskins.

'Isn't there anyone who could have gone with you?' I asked miserably.

'No,' said Dan.

He was right, of course. The rest of them had gone to war already.

'Anything else?' chirped Tom.

Dan looked around in a final check. 'That extra can beside the bollard — it might come in handy for baling. Sling it over, Tom.'

The time was running out and still I couldn't find a way to let him know . . . what? That I was proud of him? That I'd be waiting for him when he came back? Did he care whether I was or not?

Why *had* I come?

'That's it, then,' said Dan. 'Shep, up on the jetty with you. So long, Peg.'

For one moment I thought he was going to say something more, but he didn't. Instead he started up the engine; it barked, choked, and then settled into a drumming roar that beat and throbbed across field and river and ripped the quietness apart.

'Throw off that rope, Tom, and then both of you stand clear! I've got to get out of here quickly, before somebody stops me.'

And suddenly I knew what to do and why I'd come.

I waited till Tom freed the rope from the bollard, and then as he threw it to Dan and *Excalibur* swung out I took a running leap from the edge of the jetty and landed squarely in her bows. And whatever lay ahead it would be worth it, I thought, just to have seen the utter astonishment on Dan's face.

'You bloody idiot!' he shouted at me. 'You don't think for one minute I'm going to take *you* —'

'Yes, you are. Stephen's always said *Excalibur's* too heavy and awkward to sail alone.'

'You're crazy. *Crazy*! I'm putting you ashore right now.'

Rings of ripples expanded round us as he turned *Excalibur* in a circle and made back towards the jetty.

'If you do,' I said calmly, 'I'll go straight up to Stephen's house and tell his mother you've stolen the boat.'

'You wouldn't, Peg!' He didn't believe me, but he wasn't absolutely sure; not sure enough to risk it.

'Yes, I would. I *will*, if you don't take me with you. And she'll phone the coastguard and they'll stop you at the estuary — Dan, be reasonable! You need a crew!'

'Yes, Dan, you do.' Tom was yelling too. 'And Stephen said Peg was a natural at sailing, don't you remember?'

105

Dan began to laugh.

'You're a right one, Peg, you really are! The damnedest girl. If it was anybody else I wouldn't even consider it, not for a single instant —'

'Then that's all right,' I said with relief. 'Settled. Tom, you and Shep go home and tell them we're all right. Tell them we'll be back as soon as we can.' My voice was lost under the sudden sputter of the engine as Dan turned the boat again and headed down the river.

'Spare oilskins in the locker, Peg — better put them on. You don't want to get soaking wet before we even reach the sea.'

'Aye aye, sir.'

The fear was still pumping deep inside me but over it now I felt a kind of excitement, a sense that from this moment Dan and I were together, and we were part of something extraordinary.

The oilskins were Stephen's, about fourteen sizes too big. I rolled up the sleeves and trouser legs, and threw Dan an apple.

Tom was still waving from the jetty with Shep beside him as we turned the bend in the river. I waved back till he was out of sight.

'Tom said you were under starters' orders,' I remembered, as I settled down in the stern beside Dan and bit into an apple myself. 'Do you think you could tell me what they are?'

'Certainly,' said Dan. 'They're the only orders possible at a time like this. *"Steer for the sound of the guns."'*

NO HERO FOR THE KAISER

Rudolf Frank   ISBN **0 86267 200 7**

The world closed in on Jan Kubitzky on September 1914 — his fourteenth birthday. Russian soldiers, armed with guns and cannon were in the fields and similarly armed German soldiers were in the wood. Between them lay the small Polish hamlet of Kopchovka, which had been Jan's home until the day when everything in it was destroyed. When the firing stopped, only he and Flox, Vladimir the shepherd's dog, were left alive.

'*NO HERO FOR THE KAISER* is a work so remarkable that you have to wonder why it has taken so long to reach us here. The German-born author served in the 1914 war, and wrote the book from that experience. It was banned and publicly burned by Hitler in 1933. Its acclaim, we learn continues . . . Graphic, memorable . . . it's clear to see why this book was put to the flames.'

Naomi Lewis *The Observer* 1986

SWALLOW PAPERBACKS
—the current list